"It seems you've come to my rescue once again."

He held out his hand to seal the deal and gave her a crooked grin. It deepened the lines that bracketed his mouth, lending him a boyish charm.

With only a brief hesitation, she accepted his hand. Her pulse skipped a beat, then pounded erratically as her small hand was swallowed by his large warm one. It wasn't soft—it was calloused and rough like the hand of a man who worked outdoors for a living. A blush heated her cheeks, but she couldn't take her eyes off him.

She remembered him so clearly. The shape of his brow and the stone-gray color of his eyes, even the way the stubble of his beard had felt beneath her fingers. She remembered, too, the husky sound of his voice when he told her she was beautiful.

Something light and sweet slipped through her veins. An echo of a time when she'd been a giddy teenager smitten with a local boy. A time before she'd had to become a surrogate mother to her younger siblings and put her girlhood dreams away.

Books by Patricia Davids

Love Inspired

His Bundle of Love
Love Thine Enemy
Prodigal Daughter
The Color of Courage
Military Daddy
A Matter of the Heart
A Military Match
A Family for Thanksgiving
*Katie's Redemption
*The Doctor's Blessing
*An Amish Christmas

*Brides of Amish Country

Love Inspired Suspense

A Cloud of Suspicion
Speed Trap

PATRICIA DAVIDS

After thirty-five years as a nurse, Pat has hung up her stethoscope to become a full-time writer. She enjoys spending her new free time visiting her grandchildren, doing some long-overdue yard work and traveling to research her story locations. She resides with her husband in Wichita, Kansas. Pat always enjoys hearing from her readers. You can visit her on the web at www.patriciadavids.com.

An Amish Christmas
Patricia Davids

Steeple
Hill®

Published by Steeple Hill Books™

STEEPLE HILL BOOKS

Steeple
Hill®

Recycling programs
for this product may
not exist in your area.

ISBN-13: 978-0-373-81515-9

AN AMISH CHRISTMAS

Copyright © 2010 by Patricia Macdonald

www.SteepleHill.com

Printed in U.S.A.

Be wise in the way you act toward outsiders; make the most of every opportunity. Let your conversation be always full of grace, seasoned with salt, so that you may know how to answer everyone.

—*Colossians* 4: 5, 6

This book is dedicated with great affection to my readers. Without you I'm just talking to myself.

Chapter One

"Our school program will be so much fun. We're going to do a play and sing songs. I have a poem to recite all by myself. I can't wait for Christmas." Eight-year-old Anna Imhoff leaned out the side of their Amish buggy to let the breeze twirl a ribbon she held in her hand.

Karen Imhoff listened to her little sister's excited prattle with only half an ear. Christmas was still eight weeks away. There were more pressing problems on Karen's plate, like buying shoes for three growing children, her father's mounting medical bills and finding a job until he was fully recovered.

Anna sat back and grabbed Karen's sleeve. "Look, there's a dead man."

Before Karen could respond to Anna's startling comment, the horse pulling the buggy shied violently, then bolted. Caught off guard, Karen was thrown back against the leather seat as the mare lunged forward. Anna screamed at the top of her lungs. Her brothers in the backseat began yelling. The horse plunged ahead even faster.

Regaining her balance, Karen grasped the loose reins. She braced her feet against the floorboards and pulled back hard. "Whoa, Molly, whoa!"

Molly paid no heed. The buggy bounced and swayed violently as the mare charged down the farm lane. Mud thrown up by her hooves splattered Karen's dress and face. Gritty dirt mixed with the acid tang of fear in her mouth.

Anna, still screaming, threw her arms around Karen's waist, further hampering her efforts to gain control. The horse had to be stopped before they reached the highway at the end of the lane or upended in the ditch.

Muscles burning, Karen fought Molly's headlong plunge. A quarter of a mile flew past before Molly gave in. The horse slowed and came to a stop a few feet shy of the highway just as a red pickup zipped past. The brown mare tossed her head once more but didn't seem inclined to run again. Karen sent up a heartfelt prayer of thanks for their deliverance then took stock of her passengers.

Anna, with her face buried in the fabric of her sister's dress, maintained her tight grip. "I don't like to go fast. Don't do that again."

Karen comforted her with a quick hug and loosened the child's arms. "I won't. I promise."

Turning to check on her brothers, Karen asked, "Jacob? Noah? Are you all right?"

Fourteen-year-old Jacob retrieved his broad-brimmed black hat from the floor, dusted it off and jammed it on his thick, wheat-colored hair. "I'm fine. I didn't know Molly could move like that."

Ten-year-old Noah sat slumped down beside his brother. He held his hat onto his head in a tight grip with both hands. The folded brim made it look like a bonnet over his red curls. He said, "That was *not* fun."

"I thought it was," Jacob countered. "What spooked her?"

"I'm not sure." Karen's erratic heartbeat gradually slowed to a normal pace.

Brushing at the mud on her dress, Anna said, "Maybe Molly was scared of the dead man."

"What dead man?" Noah leaned forward eagerly.

"The one back there." Anna pointed behind them. They all twisted around to look. Karen saw only an empty lane.

Jacob scowled at his little sister. "I don't see anything. You're making that up."

"I am not. You believe me, don't you, Karen?"

Hugging the tearful child, Karen wasn't sure

what to believe. Anna had been the only survivor of the buggy and automobile crash that had killed their mother, two sisters and their oldest brother four years earlier. The child worried constantly about death taking another member of her family.

Karen looked into Anna's eyes. "I'm sure you saw something. A plastic bag or a bundle of rags perhaps."

Jacob, impatient as ever, said, "There's nothing back there. Let's go. I don't want to be late for school."

"We can't leave him there," Anna insisted, her lower lip quivering ominously.

Noah started to climb out. "I don't mind being late. I'll go look."

Forestalling him, Karen said, "No. We'll all go back."

Anna could easily become hysterical and then they would get nowhere. It was better to show the child that she had been mistaken. After that, Karen could drop the children at their one-room schoolhouse and hurry to her interview at Bishop Zook's home. It wouldn't do to be late for such an important meeting.

When the wedding banns had been announced for the current schoolteacher, Karen knew it meant a new teacher would have to be hired. With money tight in the Imhoff household the job would be perfect for Karen and bring in much-needed funds.

The church-district elders were speaking to teaching applicants this morning. She had to be there. But first she needed to convince Anna they didn't have a dead man on their lane.

Turning the horse around, Karen sent her walking back the way they had come. As they neared the start of their reckless run Molly balked, throwing up her head and snorting.

Not wishing to have a repeat of the mad dash, Karen said, "Jacob, take the lines."

He scrambled over the seat back to sit beside her. After handing him the driving reins Karen stepped down from the buggy. Her sturdy black shoes sank into the ground still soft from last night's rain.

The morning sun, barely over the horizon, had started to burn away the fog lingering in the low-lying farm fields. Where the sunlight touched the high wooded hillsides it turned the autumn foliage to burnished gold and scarlet flame. A breeze tugged at the ribbons of Karen's *kapp* and brought with it the smell of damp grasses and fallen leaves.

Walking briskly back toward their farmhouse, she scanned the shallow ditch beside the road without seeing anything unusual. Turning around in the road, she looked at the children and raised her arms. "I don't see anything."

"Farther back," Anna yelled.

Dropping her hands, Karen shook her head, but started walking. Anna had been leaning out her side of the carriage. She would have had a good view of the ditch. Karen had been paying attention to the problems facing her family and not to the road. A mistake she would not make again.

A few yards farther along the lane she caught a glimpse of something white in the weeds. At first she thought she'd been right and it was a bundle of cloth or a stray plastic bag caught in the brush. Then the breeze brought her a new smell—the sickly metallic odor of blood. A low moan made her jump like a startled rabbit.

Taking a few hesitant steps closer, she saw a man sprawled on his back, his body almost completely hidden in the grass and wild sumac. His face looked deathly pale beneath close-cropped black hair. Blood had oozed from an ugly gash on the side of his head.

In an instant, Karen was transported back to that terrible day when she had stood beside the remains of the smashed buggy where her mother and sisters lay dead and her brother lay dying.

She squeezed her eyes shut. Pressing her hands to her face, she whispered, "Not again, Lord, do not ask this of me."

"Did you find something?" Noah yelled.

Jerked back to the present, Karen shouted, "Stay there!"

She approached the downed man with caution. He was an *Englischer* by the look of his clothes. The muddy white shirt he wore stretched tightly across his chest and broad shoulders while his worn jeans hugged a lean waist and muscular thighs. Oddly, both his shoes were missing.

He moaned, and she moved to kneel at his side. "Sir? Sir, can you hear me?"

"It *is* a dead man!" Noah stood on the roadway looking down with wide eyes.

She scowled at her brother. "He is not dead. I told you to wait in the buggy."

"Are you sure he isn't dead?" The boy's voice brimmed with excitement.

Laying a hand on the man's cheek, Karen became alarmed by how cold his skin was. He might not be dead, but he wasn't far from it. "Run to the phone shack and call for help. Do you know how to do that?"

Noah nodded. "*Ja,* I dial 9-1-1."

"*Goot.* Hurry."

She watched her brother climb over the fence and head across the muddy field of corn stubble. Their Amish church forbade telephones in the homes of the members, but did allow a community telephone. It was located at a midway point between their home and two neighboring Amish farms.

Jacob brought the buggy up. When Molly drew alongside the ditch, she snorted and sidled away. Apparently, she didn't care for the smell of blood. That must have been what frightened her in the first place. Jacob held her in check.

Karen looked up at him, "Go get Papa."

"We can't leave you," Anna protested.

Jacob drew himself up bravely. "I should stay."

Shaking her head, Karen said, "I'll be fine. Just go. And bring some quilts. This poor man is freezing."

Jacob slapped the reins sharply and sent Molly racing up the lane toward the farmhouse. Settling herself beside the injured man, Karen took one of his hands and began to rub it between her own. How had he come to be here?

He groaned and moved restlessly. She squeezed his hand. "You will be okay, sir. My family has gone to get help."

He responded by turning his face toward her. His eyes fluttered open. They were as gray as rain clouds. Encouraged, Karen continued talking to him and rubbing his hand. "My name is Karen Imhoff and this is our farm. Can you tell me who you are?"

He mumbled something. Leaning forward, she positioned her ear near his mouth. His faint, shaky whisper sounded like, "Cold."

She quickly unbuttoned her coat. Pulling it off, she tucked it around him. Raising his shoulders slightly, she scooted beneath him so his head rested on her lap and not the chilly ground. It wouldn't help much. His clothes were wet from the rain as was the cold ground he was lying on. Using the corner of her apron, she folded it into a pad and pressed it against the wound on his head.

He moaned again, opened his eyes and focused on her face. "Help me."

His voice was barely audible but the words he whispered were the same words, the last words, her brother Seth had uttered. She cupped the *Englischer*'s face, trying to infuse him with her own strength. "Help is coming. Be strong."

Please, God, do not make me watch him die as I did Seth. Save this man if it is Your will.

With her free hand she stroked his face, offering him what comfort she could. The stubble on his cheeks rasped against her fingertips, sending an unexpected shiver zipping along her nerve endings.

His sharply chiseled features were deeply tanned, but his underlying pallor gave his skin a sickly color. His hair lay dark and thick where it wasn't matted with blood. Dark brows arched finely over his pain-filled eyes.

Raising an unsteady hand to touch her face, he fixed her with a desperate gaze and whispered, "Don't leave me."

Grasping his cold fingers, she pressed them against her cheek. He might die, but he would not die alone. "I won't leave you. I promise."

"You're...so beautiful." His voice faded. His arm went limp and dropped from her grasp.

Karen tensed. His life couldn't slip away now, not when help was so close. She shook him and spoke firmly. "Listen to me. Help is coming. You must hang on."

"Hang on...to you," he mumbled.

Tears sprang to her eyes. "Stay with me. Let God be your strength. Hold fast to Him."

After several slow breaths, he said, "Yea, though I walk...through...the—"

She took up the rest of the Twenty-third Psalm for him. *"Through the valley of the shadow of death, I will fear no evil: for thou art with me; thy rod and thy staff they comfort me. Thou preparest a table before me in the presence of mine enemies: thou anointest my head with oil; my cup runneth over."*

She glanced toward the farm. Where was her

father? What was taking so long? Desperately, she prayed help would come in time for the man she held.

Clearing her throat of its tear-choked tightness, she finished the psalm with a voice that shook. *"Surely goodness and mercy shall follow me all the days of my life: and I will dwell in the house of the LORD for ever."*

Please let Your words bring him comfort, Lord.

It seemed like hours, but finally the buggy came rattling to a stop beside her once more. Her father climbed out gingerly. His left arm rested in a sling with a cast to his shoulder.

He was dressed in dark trousers and a dark coat. His plain clothes, long beard and black felt hat proclaimed him a member of the Amish church. His calm demeanor bolstered Karen's lagging spirits.

"What is this, daughter? Anna is wailing about a dead man." Eli Imhoff pulled a bundle of blankets from the seat. Jacob remained in the buggy, controlling the restless horse.

Looking to her father in relief, she said, "We found him like this, Papa. He is badly hurt."

"I saw him first," Anna said, making sure everyone understood her contribution.

Eli's eyes grew round behind his wire-rimmed glasses. "An *Englischer?*"

"*Ja.* He is so cold. I sent Noah to the telephone to call for help."

Eli stroked his gray-streaked beard, then nodded. "It was the right thing to do. Let us pray he lives until the English ambulance comes."

As they spread more covers over the man Noah came racing back. He stopped in the lane and braced his hands on his thighs, breathing heavily. "Is he dead yet?"

"No, and he will not die," Karen stated so firmly that both her brothers and her father gave her odd looks.

She didn't care. She had seen too much death. She wanted this man to live. "Surly God has not led us to him only to snatch his life away."

"We cannot know *Gotte wille,*" her father chided.

God's will was beyond human understanding, but Karen prayed He would show His mercy to this unknown man.

"How did he get here?" Jacob asked getting down from the buggy. He handed off the reins to his younger brother. Noah didn't seem to mind. He stood at Molly's side transfixed by the sight of the stricken man.

"Perhaps he was injured on the road and walked this far before he collapsed," Eli suggested.

Squatting by the stranger's feet, Jacob shook his

head. "He didn't walk. The bottoms of his socks aren't even muddy."

They all glanced at each other as the implications sank in. Someone had dumped this man and left him to die. Karen grew sick at the idea of such cruelty and tightened her hold on him.

Eli looked at his children and spoke sternly. "This is a matter for the English sheriff. It is outsider business. We must not become involved. Do all of you understand this?"

The boys and Anna nodded. Jacob stepped away and began walking along the ditch toward the highway. Eli scowled at him, but didn't call him back. A dozen yards down the road Jacob stopped and dropped to his haunches. Karen thought she heard the faint sound of chimes for a second but then nothing more.

Eli called out to Jacob. "Did you find something?"

"Tire tracks from a car, that's all." Rising, Jacob shoved both his hands in his pockets, glanced over his shoulder and then kept walking.

In the distance, Karen heard the sound of a siren approaching at last. Her father laid a hand on her shoulder. "I will go to the highway to show the English where they are needed."

When her father and Noah had driven away, Karen looked down at her stranger. His eyes were open, but his stare was blank. Cupping his cheek, she smiled at him. "Rest easy. Help is almost here."

At the sound of her voice, he focused on her face. He tried to speak, but no words came out. His breath escaped in a deep sigh, and his eyes closed once more.

She bit her lip as she tightened her hold on him. "Just a little longer. You can do it."

Within moments the sheriff's SUV and an ambulance arrived, stopping a few feet away. Her father and Noah followed them. One of the paramedics brought his gear and dropped to his knees beside Karen. "I'll take over now, miss."

She had to let them do their job, but she didn't want to let go of her stranger. She had promised him she wouldn't leave him. God had brought her to this man's side in his hour of need. A deep feeling of responsibility for him had taken hold in her heart, but she realized her job was done.

She cupped his cheek one last time. "You will be fine now."

Rising, she stepped aside praying she had spoken the truth.

Shaking out her damp, muddy skirt, Karen crossed her arms against the chill morning air. With trepidation she saw the sheriff turned his attention her way. He was intimidating, with his gun strapped to his hip and his badge glinting on the front of his leather jacket. Sheriff Nick Bradley was English, but he had family who had remained Plain. Members of Karen's church believed him to be a fair and impartial officer of the law and friendly toward the Amish.

Stopping in front of her, he pushed his tan hat up with one finger. "Tell me exactly what happened here this morning, Miss Imhoff."

He took notes as she answered his questions and then talked to each of the children separately. Karen barely listened to her siblings' accounts. Her entire attention was focused on the man being cared for by the emergency personnel.

Her fingers itched to touch the *Englischer*'s face again. She wanted to reassure him, and herself, that he was going to be all right.

The sheriff followed Jacob to where he'd found the tire tracks, took pictures and placed yellow plastic markers at the site. When he finished, he approached Karen's father. "Mr. Imhoff, the children can go on to school, but I may have more questions for them later."

Papa nodded, but Karen could tell he wasn't pleased. This was outsider business. Papa wanted nothing to do with it. The children, on the other hand, shared excited looks. They would have plenty to tell their friends when they finally got to school. Within a day everyone in the community would know what had taken place on the Imhoff farm this morning.

One of the ambulance crew returned Karen's coat and then loaded their patient into the ambulance. As she slipped the wool jacket on, she felt the stranger's warmth surround her. Lifting the collar to her face, she breathed in the spicy-woodsy scent that clung to the dark wool.

His fate was out of her hands now. As the emergency vehicle drove away, she realized she would never see her *Englischer* again.

Chapter Two

John wiped the last trace of shaving lather from his neck with one of the hospital's coarse white towels. The face staring back at him remained as unfamiliar today as the new shoes on his feet.

How could a man forget what he looked like? How could he forget who he was, his own name?

Turning on the water, he rinsed the blue disposable blade. He knew how to use a razor but not where he'd purchased his last one or what brand he preferred. Things every man knew. It seemed only the personal parts of his memory were missing. It was the most frustrating part of his condition.

Traumatic amnesia his doctors called it. Those two words seemed woefully inadequate to describe the entity that had swallowed his life the way a black hole swallowed a star without letting a single ray of light escape.

He almost laughed at the absurdity of his thought. He could remember that weird trivial fact but not his own name. How ridiculous was that?

His doctors said his memory would return in time. They told him not to force it. Yet after eight days his past remained a blank slate. He was sick of hearing their reassurances.

"I'd like to put them in my shoes and see if they could take their own advice," he muttered as he put away his razor. Chances were good they'd be doing the same thing he was. Relentlessly trying to make himself remember.

Looking up, he stretched his hand toward the likeness in the mirror and forced a smile to his stiff lips. "Hello, my name is…"

Nothing.

Nothing came to mind this morning just as nothing had come to mind for the past week. The only identity he had was the one the hospital had given him. John Doe.

Staring at the mirror, he said, "Hi, I'm Andy. Hello, I'm Bill. I'm Carl. I'm David. My name is Edward."

If he did happen on the right name would he even know it? Rage and frustration ripped through him, bringing on a crushing headache that nearly took him to his knees.

"Who am I?" he shouted. His fingers ached where they gripped the porcelain lip of the sink.

His whole life was gone. He couldn't pull a single relevant detail out of the darkness in his mind.

He touched the bandage on the side of his scalp. According to the local law enforcement, he had been beaten, dumped in a ditch and left with no wallet or identification. Every effort to identify him was under way, but with no success thus far. His fingerprints and DNA weren't in the system. No one was looking for a man fitting his description. Even TV reports and newspaper articles had failed to bring in one solid lead.

Somewhere he must have a mother, a father, maybe even a wife, but the man in the mirror had no faces or names for anyone he'd known before waking up in the hospital.

"Too bad I wasn't microchipped like—"

Like who? Like what? The thought slipped away before he could fully grasp it. His head began pounding again. The pain worsened each time he tried to concentrate.

Forced to leave the past alone, he buttoned the last button on the gray flannel shirt the hospital social worker had purchased for him. The shirt was new. The one he'd been wearing couldn't be salvaged but the jeans were the ones he'd been found in. They fit well enough, although he'd lost some weight. Eating seemed so unimportant.

A knock sounded at the door to his room. He

moved to sit on the edge of his bed and winced at the pain in his bruised ribs. Someone had planted a kick on two in his side after they'd split his skull. He said, "Come in."

The door swung open, revealing a tall, blond man in a sheriff's uniform. John had been expecting Nick Bradley, the officer in charge of his case.

Sheriff Bradley said, "Are you ready?"

"As ready as I can be. Thanks for giving me a lift."

John was being discharged. After a week and a day of testing and probing he'd been declared fit. Physically, he was in good shape so the hospital had no reason to keep him.

Mentally? That was a different story. Leaving this room suddenly seemed more daunting than anything he could imagine. How did he start over when he had no point to start over from?

No, that wasn't exactly true. He had one point of reference. His life started a week ago in a ditch outside the town of Hope Springs, Ohio. That was where he had to go.

"Are you sure this is what you want to do?" The sheriff clearly wasn't in favor of John's plan.

"I must have been in Hope Springs for a reason. Seeing the place might trigger something. Besides, it's all I have."

"I still think you'd be better off staying here

in Millersburg, but I can see you aren't going to change your mind."

Reaching into his breast pocket, Sheriff Bradley withdrew a thick white envelope. He held it out. "My cousin Amber lives in Hope Springs. She's a nurse-midwife there. She knows about your situation. She wanted me to give you this."

"What is it?" John reached for the envelope.

"Her church took up a collection for you."

John opened the package and found himself staring at nearly a thousand dollars. Overwhelmed by the generosity of people he didn't know, he blinked hard. Tears stung the back of his eyes. He hadn't cried since—

It was there, just at the back of his mind, a feeling of grief, a feeling of overwhelming sadness. But why or for whom he had no idea. The harder he tried to concentrate on the feeling the faster it slipped away.

He forced himself to focus on the present. "Please tell your cousin how grateful I am."

"You can tell her yourself when you see Doc White to get your stitches out."

After gathering his few belongings together, John bid the nursing staff farewell and slipped into the passenger's seat of the squad car parked in front of the hospital. Within minutes they were outside the city and cruising along a narrow ribbon of black asphalt.

The highway rose and fell over gentle hills, past manicured farms and occasional stands of thick woodlands. Looking out the window he saw herds of dairy cattle near the fences. The cows barely glanced up at their passing. A half-dozen times they came upon black buggies pulled by briskly trotting horses. Each vehicle sported a bright orange triangle on the back warning motorists it was a slow-moving vehicle.

John waited for something, anything, to look familiar. He held tight to the hope that returning to where he had been found would jog his absent memory. As they finally rolled into the neat small town of Hope Springs he was once again doomed to disappointment. Nothing looked familiar.

Sheriff Bradley pulled up in front of a Swiss-chalet-styled inn and said, "This is the only inn in town. The place is run by an Amish woman named Emma Wadler. The rooms are clean but nothing fancy."

Now that he was actually at his destination, John struggled to hide his growing fears. How would he go about searching for answers? Was he going to stand on the street corner and ask each person who walked by if he looked familiar? When the sheriff got out, John forced himself to follow.

A bell over the doorway sounded as the men walked into the building. The place was cozy, charming and decorated with beautifully carved wooden furniture. An intricately pieced, colorful quilt hung over the massive stone fireplace at one end of the lobby. A display of jams for sale sat near the front door.

Behind the counter stood a small woman in blue Amish garb. Her red-brown hair was neatly parted down the middle and pulled back under a white bonnet. She was talking to someone inside a room behind the desk. She glanced toward the men and said, "I will be with you in a minute, gentlemen."

John watched her eyes closely for the slightest sign of recognition. There was none.

Turning her attention back to the person inside her office, she said, "I would gladly send overflow guests to your farm, cousin. It would be much better than telling them they must go to Millersburg or to Sugarcreek."

A woman replied, "We have spare rooms and as long as they don't mind living plain it will work. The extra money would be most welcome. If I can get *Dat* to agree to it, that is."

There was something pleasing about the unseen woman's voice. He enjoyed the singsong cadence. Her accent made *will* sound like *vil* and *welcome* sound like *vellcom*. It was familiar somehow.

The grandfather clock in the corner began to

chime the hour. John reached into the front pocket of his jeans, but found it empty.

Confused, he looked down. Something belonged there. Something was missing.

"What can I do for you, Sheriff?"

John turned around as the inn owner began a conversation with Nick. The hidden woman came out of the office and headed for the front door. She wore a dark blue dress beneath a heavy coat. An Amish cap covered her blond hair. Slender and tall, she moved with unhurried steps and innate grace. When she happened to glance in his direction, John's breath froze in his chest. His heart began thudding wildly.

Rushing across the room, he grabbed her arm in a crushing grip. "I know you. What's my name? Who am I?"

Karen recoiled in shock when a man grabbed her arm and began shouting at her. She threw up one hand to protect herself and tried to twist out of his grasp.

"Tell me who I am," he shouted again, his face only inches from hers.

A second later, the sheriff was between her and her assailant. Pushing the man back, Sheriff Bradley said, "John, what do you think you're doing?"

"I know her. I know her face. She knows who I am," he insisted, pointing at Karen.

By this time, Emma had rounded the counter and reached Karen's side, adding another body between Karen and the angry man. "Cousin, are you all right?"

Rubbing her forearm, Karen nodded. "I'm fine."

Karen glanced at the man and recognition hit. This was her *Englischer,* the man she had discovered lying injured beside their lane. That recognition must have shown on her face.

His eyes widened with hope. "You know me, right? You know my name."

She shook her head. "*Nee.* I do not."

The sheriff spoke calmly but firmly. "John, this is Karen Imhoff. She's the one who found you."

His body went slack in the sheriff's hold. The color drained from his face as the hope in his eyes died. His look of pain and disappointment twisted her heart into a knot.

She said, "It was my little sister who spotted you lying in the weeds."

His eyes suddenly narrowed. "I was told I was unconscious when the paramedics arrived. How is it that I know your face?"

As her racing heart slowed and her fright abated, Karen took a step closer. He was alive and standing here before her. Joy gladdened her heart. He had been in her thoughts and prayers unceasingly. It took all her willpower not to reach out and touch his face.

She said, "You opened your eyes and spoke to me. You told me you were cold. I put my coat over you."

The sheriff released his grip on John. "She doesn't know anything about you. I've already questioned her and her family. There's no connection between you."

A look of resignation settled over John's features. He raised a hand to his forehead and rubbed it as if trying to rub away pain. "I'm sorry if I hurt or frightened you, Miss Imhoff. Please forgive me."

He did not remember her holding him close. Perhaps that was for the best. She had come to the aid of a stranger, nothing more. The rest, the closeness, the connection she felt with him, those things would remain in her secret daydreams.

"You are forgiven," she said quietly. What she didn't understand was why he had insisted that she tell him his own name.

The sheriff looked toward the innkeeper. "Sorry for the disturbance, Emma. This is John Doe, the man found injured near here a week ago. John has amnesia."

"What does this mean?" Karen asked, unfamiliar with the English term.

John's eyes locked with hers. Once again she felt a stirring bond with him deep in her bones. It was suddenly hard to breathe.

He said, "It means I can't remember anything that happened before I was hurt. Not even my own name, but I remember your face and the sound of your voice."

Compassion drenched Karen's heart and brought the sting of tears to her eyes. His suffering had not ended when the ambulance took him away from her.

Sheriff Bradley said, "John needs a room for a little while, Emma. He doesn't have any ID so I came to vouch for him in person."

Emma said, "I'm sorry, I don't have anything available for a week. I just rented my last room an hour ago. You know the quilt auction begins tomorrow. It runs for several days, and then there is the Sutter wedding. By next Friday I will have a room."

Clearly upset with himself, Nick said, "I'm sorry, John. I should have called ahead. They aren't normally booked up here. I know you had your heart set on staying in Hope Springs. I didn't even think about the auction being this week. I'll take you back to Millersburg. We can find a place for you there."

"We have a room to let." Karen's desire to help John overrode her normally good sense. He was a stranger lost in a strange land. He needed her help today as much as he'd needed it the day she found him.

His eyes narrowed as he stared at her. Karen bit the corner of her lip. What had she done? She should have discussed this with her father first, but she had already made the offer and couldn't withdraw it.

When she explained things her father would realize the benefits of this additional income. Especially after she had failed to get the teaching job.

Their family's income had been severely limited following her father's injury a month earlier. A farrier couldn't shoe horses with his arm in a cast. There were still medical bills that needed to be paid in addition to their everyday expenses.

She would point out all those things, but she knew he would not be pleased if she brought this man and his English trouble into their house.

She fidgeted under John's unwavering gaze. Finally, he said, "Your farm was the first place I had planned to visit when I arrived. Renting a room there makes sense."

"For a week," she stressed. "After that, Emma will have a place for you here."

"It seems you've come to my rescue once again." He held out his hand to seal the deal and gave her a crooked grin. It deepened the lines that bracketed his mouth, lending him a boyish charm.

With only a brief hesitation, she accepted his hand. Her pulse skipped a beat then pounded erratically as her small hand was swallowed by his large, warm one. It wasn't soft, it was calloused and rough like the hand of a man who worked outdoors for a living. A blush heated her cheeks, but she couldn't take her eyes off of him.

She remembered him so clearly. The shape of his brow and the stone-gray color of his eyes, even the way the stubble of his beard had felt beneath her fingers. She remembered, too, the husky sound of his voice when he had told her she was beautiful.

Something light and sweet slipped through her veins. An echo of a time when she'd been a giddy teenager smitten with a local boy. A time before she'd had to become a surrogate mother to her younger siblings and put her girlhood dreams away.

Thoughts of the children brought her back to earth with a thud. She pulled her hand away from John. This man was an outsider and thus forbidden to her. She had offered him a room to rent for a week and nothing more. Her strange fascination with him had to stop, and quickly.

Gesturing toward the door, she said, "I must get home."

He said, "I don't have any sort of transportation. May I hitch a ride with you?"

Oh, *Dat* really wasn't going to like this, but what could she do? She gave a stiff smile. "Of course."

Emma asked quietly, "Karen, are you sure about this?"

Pretending a bravery she didn't feel, Karen answered, "Yes. Goodbye, cousin, I will see you at Katie's wedding next Thursday."

Emma didn't look happy, but she nodded. "Give *Onkel* Eli my best."

John shook hands with the sheriff, who promised to check up on him soon, and then followed Karen out the door. Her nervousness increased tenfold as he fell into step beside her.

He was taller than she thought he would be. She had been called a beanpole all her life, but he stood half a head taller than she did. She felt delicate next to his big frame. It was a strange feeling. Spending the next half hour in this man's company in the close confines of her buggy might prove to be awkward.

After unlatching Molly's lead from the hitching rail, Karen was surprised when John took her elbow to help her climb in the buggy. She was used to taking care of herself and everyone else. It had been a long time since someone had wanted to take care of her.

John walked slowly around the front of the horse. Raising a hand, he patted the mare's neck and made a soothing sound as he cast a critical eye over the animal. "She's got good conformation. She's a Standardbred, right?"

"*Ja*. You know about horses?"

"I think I do." He scratched Molly under the earpiece of her headstall. The mare tipped her head and rubbed against his hand in horsy bliss.

It seemed he could charm horses as well as foolish Amish maids. She said, "We must be going."

He nodded and climbed into the buggy beside her. Karen turned the horse and sent her trotting briskly down the street. The fast clatter of Molly's hooves matched almost exactly the rapid pounding of Karen's heart. It was going to be a long ride home.

Clucking her tongue, she slapped the reins against Molly's rump, making the mare go faster. The sooner they reached the farm, the better.

Karen's skin prickled at John's nearness. He had been in her thoughts and prayers constantly since that day. The special connection she'd felt between them had not diminished. She had wondered who he was and if he had gotten better. She'd wondered, too, if he had a wife to care for him. She had prayed he wasn't alone.

Now, he had come back to her.

He had been helpless as a babe that day, a man in need of tender care. The vibrant man beside her now was anything but helpless. What had she been thinking to invite him into her home?

He remained silent beside her as they drove out of town. Covertly, Karen glanced his way often, but he was scanning the countryside and paying her no mind. The cold, rainy weather of last week had give way to sunny days of Indian summer. The countryside was aglow with the vibrant hues of autumn. It should have been a pleasant ride. Instead, Karen felt ready to jump out of her skin.

After twenty minutes of listening only to the clip-clop of Molly's hooves and the creaking of the buggy, John spoke at last. "This isn't the way I came into Hope Springs with Sheriff Bradley. What road is this?"

She glanced at him. "It's called Pleasant View Road. Does that mean something to you?"

He shook his head. "Nothing more than it's well named. Where does it lead?"

"It makes a wide loop and goes back to Highway 39 about ten miles south of here. From there, you can go to the town of Sugarcreek or over to Millersburg."

"Why would someone like me be on this road?"

Shrugging her shoulders, Karen said, "Because you were lost?"

He barely smiled. "If I wasn't then, I am now."

Her curiosity about him couldn't be contained any longer. "The sheriff called you John Doe, but that is not your name?"

"No. John Doe is a name they give to any man who is unidentified. It's usually given to a dead body, but fortunately for me I'm still alive."

"This amnesia—will it go away?"

He stared into the distance for a long time before answering. Finally, he said, "The doctors tell me my memory may come back on its own or it may not come back at all."

"It must be awful." Her heart went out to him.

His attention swung back to her. "What can you tell me about the day you found me?"

"I was driving my younger brothers and sister to school. Normally they walk, but I had an appointment that day. I thought it would be easier just to drop them on my way."

"Did you notice anything unusual that morning?"

Giving him a look of disbelief, she asked, "You mean other than finding an unconscious man by the side of the road?"

That brought a small, lopsided grin to his face, easing the tension between them. "Yes, other than finding me in a ditch, did you notice anything that was unusual or out of place?"

"Nothing." She wanted to help him, but she

couldn't. "The sheriff has already asked us these questions."

Leaning forward, he braced his elbows on his knees and clasped his hands together in front of him. "I just thought you might have remembered something new since that day. Maybe you heard the sound of a car or voices. Do you have a dog?"

"We do not."

"Do you remember hearing anything during the night?"

"*Nee,* I heard nothing unusual. I'm sorry."

He pressed his lips into a thin line and nodded in resignation. "That's okay. Are we close to your farm?"

"It's not far now. You will see the sign."

"Tell me about yourself, Karen Imhoff." He fixed her with an intense stare that brought the blood rushing to her face.

"There is not much to tell. As you can see I am Amish. My mother passed away some years ago so I am in charge of my father's house."

"What did you mean when you told the innkeeper that your lodgers would have to live plain?"

He really didn't know? Grinning, she said, "You will be wanting your money back when you find out."

"Do you give refunds?"

"*Nee,* when money goes into my pocket it does not come out easily."

"Okay, then tell me gently."

"Plain living means many things. No electricity and all that comes with it. No television, no computers, no radio."

"Wow. What did I get myself into?"

She glanced at him, but he was smiling and didn't look upset. Feeling oddly happy, she said, "We go to bed early and we get up early. My father farms and is the local farrier, but we will not put you to work shoeing horses."

"Thanks for the small favor."

"I have two brothers, Jacob is fourteen and Noah is ten. I also have a sister. Anna is eight."

His mood dimmed. "I wonder if I have brothers or sisters."

"You are welcome to some of mine," she offered, hoping to make him smile again. It worked.

"Don't you find it hard to live without electricity?"

"Why would I? People lived happily without electricity for many centuries."

"Good point. Why don't the Amish use it?"

"We are commanded by the Bible to live separate from the world. Having electricity joins us to the world in a way that is bad for us. We do not shun all modern things. Only those things that do not work to keep our families and our communities strong and close together."

"I still don't get it."

"That is because you are an *Englischer*."

"I'm a what?" He frowned.

"English. An outsider. Our word for those who are not of our faith. This is our lane."

Karen slowed the horse and turned onto the narrow road where a large white sign with a black anvil painted on it said, Horse Shoeing. Closed Wednesdays. The word *Wednesdays* was currently covered by a smaller plaque that said Until Further Notice.

John sat up straighter. "Where did you find me?"

"A little ways yet."

When they approached the spot, Karen drew the horse to a stop. John jumped down and walked into the knee-high winter-brown grass and shrubs along the verge of the road. The sheriff had combed the area for clues but found nothing.

Karen kept silent and waited as John made his own search. One look at his face made her realize John Doe was still a wounded man, but he was in need of more than physical care.

Chapter Three

John stared at the matted grass around his feet. No trace of the incident remained. No blood stains, no footprints, no proof that he had ever lain here.

Squatting down, he touched the grass and waited for an answer to appear. Why had he been in this place?

Had his injury been an accident or had someone deliberately tried to kill him? Had it been a robbery gone bad as the sheriff thought? No matter what the explanation, the fact remained that he'd been left here to die. The knowledge brought a sick feeling to the pit of his stomach.

Standing, he shoved his hands in his pockets and scanned the horizon. All around him lay farm fields. To the east, a wooded hill showed yellow and crimson splashes of autumn colors. A cold breeze flowed around his face. He closed his eyes and breathed deeply, hoping to trigger some hint of familiarity.

Nothing.

He searched his empty mind for some sliver of recognition and drew a blank.

He'd been so sure coming here would make him remember. This was where his old life ended. He wanted to see the scattered bits of it lying at his feet. He wanted to pick up the puzzle pieces and assemble them into something recognizable. Only there was nothing to pick up.

Now what?

He glanced toward the buggy where Karen sat. He'd been found on her land. Did she know more than she was letting on? Sitting prim and proper with her white head covering and somber clothes, it was hard to imagine she could be involved in something as ugly as an assault. But what did he know about her, anyway? Maybe coming here had been a mistake. He would proceed with caution until he knew more about her and her family.

She watched him silently. As their eyes met, he read sympathy in their depths. Turning away he bit the inside of his cheek until he tasted blood. The pain overrode the sting of unshed tears. He didn't want sympathy. He wanted answers.

John didn't know how long he stood staring into the distance. Eventually, Molly grew impatient and began pawing the ground. He glanced at Karen. She drew her coat tight under her chin. He realized the sun was going down and it was getting colder.

Walking back to the buggy, he said, "I'm sorry. I didn't mean to keep you waiting so long."

She smiled softly. "I don't mind, but I think Molly wants her grain."

"Then we should go." Walking around to the opposite side he climbed in.

"Did you remember anything?" she asked.

"No." He stared straight ahead as his biggest fear slithered from the dark corner of his mind into the forefront. What if he never remembered? What if this blankness was all he'd ever have?

No, he refused to accept that. He had family, friends, a job, a home, a car, a credit card, a bank account, something that proved he existed. His life was out there waiting for him. He wouldn't give up until he found it.

When they reached the farmyard, Karen drew the mare to a stop in front of a two-story white house. A welcoming porch with crisp white railings and wide steps graced the front. Three large birdhouses sat atop poles around the yard ringed with flowerbeds. Along one side of the house several clotheslines sagged under the weight of a dozen pairs of pants, dresses, shirts, socks and sheets all waving in the cool evening breeze.

Across a wide expanse of grass stood a large

red barn and several outbuildings. In the corral, a pair of enormous caramel-colored draft horses munched on a round hay bale with a dozen smaller horses around them. Molly whinnied to announce her return. The herd replied in kind.

John swallowed hard against the pain in his chest. What did his home look like? Was someone waiting to greet him? Were they worried sick about where he was? If that was the case, why hadn't they come forward?

Something of what he was thinking must have shown on his face. Karen laid her hand on his. The warmth of her touch flooded through him.

Sympathy had prompted Karen's move. She saw and understood the struggle he was going through. "Let God be your solace, John. He understands all that you are going through. You are not alone."

John nodded, but didn't speak.

Karen turned to get out of the buggy but froze. Her stern-faced father stood before her. He looked from John to Karen and demanded, "What is the meaning of this, daughter?"

Stepping down from the buggy, she brushed the wrinkles from the front of her dress. "Papa, this is Mr. John Doe. John, this is my father, Eli Imhoff. Papa, I have rented a room to Mr. Doe."

Eli Imhoff's dark bushy eyebrows shot up in surprise. "You have, have you?"

Karen had learned the best way to handle her father was to charge straight ahead. She switched to Pennsylvania Dutch, the German dialect normally spoken in Amish homes, knowing John would not be able to understand them. "I will show him to his room and then I will speak with you about this."

"Better late than never, I'm thinking," Eli replied in the same language.

"I'm sure you'll agree this was a *goot* idea. You know we need the money. The *dawdy haus* is sitting empty. This is only for a week, and he is paying us the same amount that Emma charges her customers."

"And if I say *nee?*"

She acquiesced demurely. "Then I shall drive him back to town. Although Emma has no room for him at her inn I'm sure he can find someplace to stay."

John spoke up. "Look, if this is a problem I can make other arrangements."

Karen crossed her arms and raised one eyebrow as she waited for her father to answer.

The frown her father leveled at her said they would hold further discussions on the matter when they were alone. Looking to John, he said, "You are welcome to stay the night."

"Thank you, sir. I promise not to be any trouble."

"You are the man my daughter found on the road, *ja?*"

"I am. I want to thank you for your help that day."

"We did naught but our Christian duty," Eli said, turning away.

As her father disappeared into the house, Karen swung back to John. "Come. You will have a house to yourself. It has its own kitchen, sitting room and bedroom. It is the *dawdy haus* but my grandparents have both passed away and it is not in use. You may take your meals with us unless you enjoy cooking."

"What is a *dawdy haus?*" John asked as he pulled his small bag from behind the buggy seat.

"It means grandfather house. Among our people it is common to add a room or home onto the farmhouse so that our elderly relatives have a place to stay. Many times we have three or four generations living together under one roof. It is our way."

"Sounds like a good way to me."

She smiled at that. "I'm glad you think so."

He swept one hand in front of him. "Lead the way."

The *dawdy haus* had been built at a right angle to the main farmhouse. It was a single-story white clapboard structure with a smaller front porch. A pair of wooden chairs flanked a small table at the far end of the porch. The outside door opened into a small mudroom. A second door led directly into the kitchen.

Karen said, "We have gas lamps. Have you ever used them before?"

"I don't know."

She cringed. "I'm sorry."

"Don't be. There's no point in tiptoeing around with your questions. Either I'll remember a thing or I won't. I won't know until you ask."

Striking a match, Karen raised it to the lamp and lit it. A soft glow filled the room, pushing back the growing darkness. She glanced at John and found him watching her intently. Suddenly, it seemed as if the two of them were cocooned alone inside the light.

The lamplight highlighted the hard planes of his face. She became acutely aware of him, of his size and the brooding look in his eyes. The tension in the room seemed to thicken. His gaze roved over her face. Her palms grew sweaty as her pulse quickened. She wondered again if she had made a serious mistake in bringing him here.

Yet, she could not have left him in Hope Springs any more than she could have passed by him in the ditch without helping. There was something about John Doe that called to her.

He tried to hide his discomfort and his

aloneness, but she saw it lurking in the depths of his eyes. He was afraid. She wanted to help him, wanted to ease his pain. He needed her.

The white bandage on his forehead stood out against his dark hair. She gave in to an over-whelming urge and reached out to touch his face. Her fingertips brushed against the gauze dressing. "Does it hurt?"

He turned his head aside. "It's nothing."

"You're forgetting that I saw the gash."

The muscles in his jaw tightened. "I've forgotten a lot of things."

She let her hand drop to her side. How foolish of her. He wasn't a stray puppy that needed her care. He was a grown man, and she was flirting with forbidden danger. For the first time in her life she understood how a moth could be drawn to the flame that would destroy it.

She must harden her heart against this weakness. "Let me show you the rest of the house."

He grasped her arm as she started to turn away. "I can manage. If I need anything I'll find you. Right now, I'd like to be alone. It's been a long day."

"Of course." She handed him the box of matches. "Be sure and turn off the gas lamps when you leave the house. There are kerosene lamps, too, if you need them. Supper will be ready in about an hour. You may join us at the table or I can bring something to you."

"If it's all the same, I'm not up to company and I'm not really hungry. Thank you, though, for everything."

Slowly, he withdrew his hand from her arm in a gentle caress. She rubbed at the warmth that remained. She must not confuse his gratitude with affection nor give in to her feelings of attraction. To do so would be unthinkable.

She mumbled, "It is our Christian duty to care for those in need. I will be back with linens and a pillow for you in a little while."

As she left the house, she paused on the porch to slow her racing pulse. Her family must not see her flustered.

She did not doubt that God had brought John Doe into her life again for a reason but that reason was hidden from her. Was it so that she might help this outsider? Or had John Doe been sent to test the strength of her faith? Would she pass such a test or would she fail?

John drew a deep breath as soon as Karen was gone. He couldn't seem to concentrate when she was near. He didn't understand why. The woman wasn't a great beauty, but she had an elegant presence he found very attractive. Perhaps it was the peace in her tranquil blue eyes or the surety with which she carried herself.

She knew exactly where she belonged in her small reclusive world while he was adrift in an ever-changing sea of turmoil that sought to swallow his sanity along with his memories. Her empathy had quickly become his lifeline. One he was afraid to let go of.

"Get real. I can't hang on the apron strings of an Amish farmer's daughter."

Pushing his attraction to her to the back of his mind, he studied the small kitchen. He was surprised to see a refrigerator. On closer inspection, it turned out to be gas not electric, but it was empty and had apparently had the gas turned off. The few drawers were filled with normal kitchen utensils. The stove was wood burning.

Did he even know how to cook?

He opened a cupboard and pulled out a heavy cast-iron skillet. Hefting it in his hand, he suddenly saw it full of sizzling trout. He saw himself setting it on a trivet, hearing murmurs of appreciation, a woman's lighthearted laughter.

He spun around to face the table knowing someone sat there, but when he did—the image vanished.

"No!"

The loss was so sharp he doubled over in pain. Who was the woman with him? His mother? A sister? A wife? Where had it taken place? When? Was it a real memory or only a figment of his imagination?

He looked at the pan he held and saw only a blackened skillet. Setting it on the stovetop he rubbed his hands on his thighs. It had been a real memory, he was sure of it. But had it been a month ago or ten years ago? It held no context. It faded before he could grasp hold and examine it.

Pulling himself together, he blew out a shaky breath. Okay, it had only been a flash. But it could mean he was on the mend.

Hope—new and crisp—flooded his body. Maybe the doctors had been right and time was all he needed. He had time. He had nothing but time.

Using the matches Karen had given him, he lit a kerosene lamp sitting on the counter and began walking through the rest of the house. The wide plank floors creaked in places as he entered the sitting room containing several chairs and a small camelback sofa. None of the furniture shouted "kick back and relax." It was utilitarian at best.

Down a narrow hallway he passed a small bathroom and noted with relief the modern fixtures. At the end of the hall he opened the door to a sparsely furnished bedroom.

The narrow bed, covered with a blue striped mattress, stood against a barren white wall. A bureau sat against the opposite wall while a delicate desk graced the corner by the window. The walls were empty of any decorations. The one chair in the room was straight-backed with a cane seat.

Crossing the wooden floor, he set the lamp on the bedside table. He stared at the thin mattress, then sat down and bounced slightly. It was one shade better than his hospital bed but only two shades softer than the floor. Apparently, the Amish didn't go in for luxury.

He lay back on the bed and folded his arms behind his head to stare at the ceiling. Was his own bedroom this bare? He waited for another spark of memory, but nothing came.

The pain in his head had settled to a dull ache he'd almost grown used to. There were pain pills in his duffel bag, a prescription filled at the hospital pharmacy, but he didn't like the idea of using them. His thinking was muddled enough without narcotics. He closed his eyes and laid one arm across his face. Slowly, the tension left his body and he dozed.

A rap on the door brought him awake. He sat up surprised to see it was fully dark beyond the window outside. Karen stood in the doorway, her arms loaded with sheets, quilts and a pillow. She asked, "Did I wake you?"

"No. I was only resting." John wasn't about to

make Karen feel bad after all that she'd done for him. He rose to take the linens from her. Their fresh sun-dried fragrance filled his nostrils.

Taking a step back, she folded her arms nervously. "I left you a plate of food on the table. You should eat. You need to regain your strength."

"Thanks." He expected her to hurry away, but she lingered.

"Is the house to your satisfaction?" she asked.

"It's great. Better than a four-star motel. That's a place where people can stay when they're traveling—if you didn't know." Did he sound like a fool or what?

An amused grin curved her full lips. "I know what a motel is. We do travel sometimes. I have even been to Florida to visit my great aunt and uncle there."

"I'll bet the horse got tired trotting all that way."

Her giggle made him smile. A weight lifted from his chest.

Composing herself, Karen said, "I took the train."

It surprised him how much he enjoyed talking to her. He asked, "Can't you fly?"

"No, my arms get too tired," she answered with a straight face.

He laughed for the first time since he'd awakened in the hospital. "I don't know Amish rules."

"We can't own automobiles, but we can hire a driver to take us places that are too far for a buggy trip. With our bishop's permission, we can travel by train or by bus and even by airplane if the conditions are warranted."

"That must be tough."

"That's the point. If it is easy to get in a car and go somewhere, to a new city or a new job, then families become scattered and the bonds that bind us together and to God become frayed and broken."

"It's an interesting philosophy."

"It is our faith, not an idea. It is the way God commands us to live. How is your headache?"

"It's gone," he said in surprise.

"I thought so. You look rested. And now you must eat before your supper gets cold."

He followed her down the hall to the kitchen. A plate covered with aluminum foil sat on the table. He peeled back the cover and the mouthwatering aroma of roast chicken and vegetables rose with the steam. His stomach growled. He was hungry. "Smells good."

He hesitated, then said, "I remembered something tonight."

Her eyes brightened. "What?"

If he shared his small victory would she think he was nuts? He didn't care if she did. He was tired of being alone.

"I've cooked trout before. I know it doesn't sound like much, but it's my first real memory. At least, I believe it was a memory."

"It is a start. We must give thanks to God."

His elation slipped a notch. Wasn't God the one who'd put him in this situation? If he were to give thanks it would have to be for remembering something important—like his name.

She said, "At least you know one more thing about yourself."

He could cook fish, he had no criminal record and he didn't crave drugs. Yeah, he was off to a roaring good start in his quest to collect personal information. Maybe tomorrow he'd find he knew how to sharpen a pencil.

Depression lowered its dark blanket over him. "Thanks for the supper."

"You are most welcome. I will expect you at our breakfast table in the morning," she stated firmly. The look in her eyes told him she was used to being the boss.

Her family would be there, people who would stare at him with pity or worse. Was he ready for that?

Not waiting for his answer, she said, "I will send Jacob to get you if you don't appear. No, I will send Noah. His endless questions will make you wish you had stayed in Hope Springs. The only way to silence him is to feed him. *Guten nacht,* John Doe."

"Good night, Karen."

The ribbons of her white bonnet fluttered over her shoulders as she spun around and headed out the door. It appeared he wouldn't be allowed to hide here in the house if she had her way.

That was okay. He wouldn't mind seeing her face across the breakfast table or at any other time. Why wasn't she married?

He reined in the thought quickly. It was none of his business. She was an attractive woman with a vibrant personality, but he was in no position to think about flexing his social skills. What if he had a wife waiting for him somewhere?

He stared at his left hand. No discernible pale band indicated he normally wore a wedding ring. It wasn't proof positive, of course. Not every married man wore a wedding band. Did he feel married?

How could he remember frying trout and not remember if he had a wife?

The creaking of a floorboard in the other room caught his attention. Was there someone in the house with him? His mouth went dry as a new fear struck.

Had someone come back to finish the job and make sure he was dead?

Chapter Four

Grabbing a knife from the drawer beside the sink, John walked slowly to the doorway of the sitting room and scoped it out. It was empty.

Was he imagining things now? He started to turn away, but another sound stopped him. He focused on the sofa just as the face of a little girl peeked over the back. The moment she saw him watching she ducked down again.

Relief made him light-headed. Karen had mentioned she had a sister. It seemed one Imhoff was too curious about him to wait until morning. He said, "I see you."

"No, you don't," came her reply.

Feeling foolish, he laid the knife on the table, then he crossed the sitting room and bent over the sofa. Looking down, he saw her huddled into a little ball. "Okay, now I see you."

Wearing a dark blue dress with a white apron

and a white bonnet identical to her older sister's she looked like a miniature Karen. She nodded and grinned. "*Ja,* now you see me."

Scrambling to her feet, she sidestepped to the other end of the sofa. "You are my dead man. I saw you in the ditch. Everyone said I made it up, but I didn't."

"I was in the ditch, but I wasn't dead."

She moved around the room trailing her fingers along the furniture. "I know. God didn't want you, either. We are just alike."

He had no idea what she was talking about. "I'm not sure we are."

"It's true," she insisted. "This house belonged to my *grossmammi.*"

"I don't know what that means."

She cocked her head sideways. "Really? It means grandmother. These are her things, but God wanted her in heaven, and she had to leave her things here."

John sat on the sofa. "Do you think your grandmother will mind that I'm using them?"

She shook her head. "She liked it when people came to visit."

He said, "My name is John. What's your name?"

"Anna."

"It's nice to meet you Anna. What did you mean when you said we are the same?"

"God didn't want me to go to heaven the day my mother died. Seth, Carol and Liz got to go to Heaven with Mama, but God didn't want me. And he didn't want you. Why do you think that is?"

"I have no idea."

She came to stand in front of him. Tipping her head to one side, she said, "Papa says it is because God has something special for me to do here on earth. I don't think it's fair, do you?"

John stared at his toes in hopes that an appropriate answer would appear. None did. He wasn't up to discussing the meaning of life with this odd child. "I think maybe you should talk to your dad or Karen about it."

"Okay. Are you going to eat all that chicken?"

"I was, but I'm willing to share."

Spinning around she bounced toward the kitchen and settled in one of the chairs. He followed her and took a seat at the head of the table. Uncovering the plate, he pushed it toward her. "I'll let you choose the piece you want."

"I like the leg, but you are the guest."

"That makes it easy because I like the thigh."

He watched her bite into his supper. "Anna, can I ask you a few questions?"

She considered his request for a moment then nodded. "Okay."

"What's with the bonnets that you and your sister wear?"

Reaching up to touch her head, she asked, "You mean our prayer *kapp?*"

"Yeah, why do you wear them? I know you do because you are Amish, but why?"

She looked at him with wide eyes. "Are you joshing me?"

"No."

"It says in the Bible that I should cover my head when I pray. I should pray all the time so I wear this all the time. Sometimes I forget to pray, but Karen reminds me. Can I ask you a question?"

"Sure."

"Why were you in our ditch?"

"I don't remember what I was doing there. I don't remember anything that happened to me before you saw me. John Doe isn't even my real name. It's a name they gave me because I can't remember my own."

Her mouth dropped open. "Now you *are* joshing me?"

Shaking his head, he smiled and said, "I wish I were."

The outside door opened and a teenage boy entered. He frowned at Anna. "You should not be here."

She rolled her eyes. "Neither should you."

"She's not causing any trouble," John said in defense of his visitor.

The boy ignored him. "Come now or I will tell *Dat*."

Anna finished her chicken and licked her fingers. "This is my brother, Jacob. He says having an *Englischer* stay here will get us all in trouble with the bishop."

John looked from Anna to her brother. "Is this true? Will my being here cause trouble?"

Jacob came into the room and took Anna by the hand. Looking at John he said, "You should leave this place."

Turning around, Jacob left, taking his little sister with him.

It seemed getting to know the Imhoff family was going to be more difficult than John had anticipated.

Karen was cooking breakfast when John knocked at the door the following morning. She hadn't had to send one of the children to wake him. After bidding him enter, she turned back to the stove and smiled as she stirred the frying potatoes. John was an early riser. That was one more thing he could add to his list about himself.

She moved the skillet off the heat. "Take a seat, Mr. Doe."

He said, "Please call me John."

Noah and Anna were already at the table sitting opposite each other but Eli and Jacob had not yet come in from the milking. Anna pointed to the chair opposite her. "Sit by Noah, John."

He settled himself into the chair she indicated and looked at the boy beside him. "You must be Noah."

Karen glanced over her shoulder to see Noah fairly bursting with curiosity.

"*Ja,* I am Noah. Is it true you can't remember your name? Not even where you came from? Do you remember that you're English or did someone tell you? How did you know how to talk? If you need to know how to use a knife and fork I can show you."

Karen caught John's eye and said, "I warned you."

While John patiently answered Noah's rapid-fire questions, Karen pulled her biscuits from the oven. Dumping them into a woven basket, she set it on the table in front of everyone.

Just then the front door opened. Her father and Jacob came in. After washing up, they took their places at the table. Karen sat down opposite John. Everyone folded their hands. Silently her father gave a blessing over the meal. He signaled he had finished by clearing his throat, then giving a brief nod to Karen. She began passing food down the table.

Eli said, "*Guder mariye,* Mr. Doe."

"Good morning, sir." John took a biscuit and

watched with a bemused expression as the children dived into their food. By the time the plate of scrambled eggs reached him only a tablespoon's worth remained.

Eli spoke to Karen. "William Yoder wants me to look at one of his draft horses this afternoon. His gelding has a split hoof. He wants my opinion on which treatment to try."

She asked, "Do you need me to drive you?"

Jacob perked up with interest. "Can I go with you, Papa?"

Karen's spoke quickly, "You have school today." Jacob was growing up fast, but she wasn't ready for him to take on their father's tough and sometimes dangerous profession before it was necessary.

Sitting back in his chair, Jacob said, "I don't see why I have to go to school now. Papa needs me at home to help him with the horses."

"You will be out of school soon enough," Karen said. "A few more months won't do you any harm."

Jacob made a sour face. "Ken Yoder has already left school. He is only two months older than me. I don't need any more schooling. I want to work with you, Papa. I want to be a farrier."

John said, "A farrier needs an education, too."

Karen looked at him in surprise. It was becoming clear he did know a thing or two about horses.

"What do you know about it?" Jacob scowled at their guest.

"Jacob." Eli's firm tone rebuked his son.

Bowing his head, Jacob mumbled, "Forgive me."

Spreading jam on a piping-hot biscuit, John said, "If the horse has a turned foot, a farrier needs a shoe to correct it for him. You would have to know how many degrees the foot was off true in order to make a shoe that brings it up to level. How thick does the shoe need to be to give such an angle? These things you learn in school."

Anna shook her head. "We don't learn horse-shoeing in school. We learn how to read and write, how to speak English and how to do our sums."

Eli smiled at her. "And did you finish your sums last night?"

Her bright face clouded over. "No, Papa."

"And why not?" Karen asked, surprised to hear Anna had neglected her homework.

"Because I went to visit John Doe."

John said, "I would have sent her back if I had known. She kept me company while I ate."

Jacob glared at John and then spoke to Karen. "See. No *goot* can come of having him stay here."

"Hush Jacob, this is not how we treat our guests," Karen said.

Pushing back from the table, Jacob got up. "The *Englischer* will only bring trouble. You will see."

He grabbed his coat and hat and headed outside, letting the door slam behind him. Eli rose, motioning to Karen to stay seated. "I will talk to the boy."

Slipping his coat over his sling, he followed Jacob outside. Embarrassed by her brother's display, Karen glanced at John.

He gave her a tight smile and said, "I'm sorry I upset him."

"It's not you." She knew what troubled her brother and her heart ached for him.

Noah spoke around a mouthful of egg. "Jacob doesn't like the English ever since the accident."

Puzzled, John asked, "What accident?"

"The accident that killed our mother, brother and sisters," Karen explained.

"That *Englischer* was drunk. He hit their buggy doing like seventy miles an hour," Noah added dramatically.

Karen was thankful Noah had not been there that day. It had been she and Jacob who came upon the terrible carnage.

Karen reached across the table to grasp Noah and Anna's hands. "We have forgiven him as God has asked us to do."

Nodding solemnly, Noah agreed. "We have."

Anna shook her head. "I don't think Jacob has."

Karen squeezed her hand. "We will pray Jacob finds forgiveness in his heart."

John asked, "What happened to the driver?"

Letting go of her siblings, Karen folded her hands in her lap. "He had barely a scratch."

Frowning slightly, John looked from the children to Karen. "How do you do that? How do you forgive someone who has done something so terrible?"

"It is our way," Karen replied. Closing her eyes, she sought the peace that forgiveness always brought her.

When she opened her eyes, she found John's gaze resting thoughtfully on her. Heat rose in her face. Hoping he hadn't noticed, she said, "Hurry up children, or you will be late to school."

In the resulting rush, Karen masked her nervousness by handing out lunch boxes, scarves and mittens. By the time the children were out the door, she had a better grip on her emotions.

John, on the other hand, looked ill at ease. The frown lines that creased his forehead yesterday were back.

Karen began picking up plates. "Would you like more coffee or more eggs?"

"I don't want to cause you extra work. Coffee is fine if you have it." He remained seated, elbows resting on the table.

"It's not extra work. Cooking is what I do all day long. Ask now or go hungry until lunch."

"Okay, more eggs would be great."

"Did you sleep well?" She pulled a bowl of fresh eggs from the refrigerator.

"Not bad."

She glanced his way. Something in the tone of his voice made her suspect he hadn't. "The bed was not to your liking?"

He shifted uncomfortably in his chair. "It wasn't that."

"Then what was it?"

"Anna mentioned that Jacob thinks your family might get in trouble for having me here."

Turning around, she folded her arms and stated as firmly as she could, "You were invited into this house. There is nothing wrong in that."

"Are you sure? Because I got the feeling your father wasn't happy to see me, either."

"Papa has agreed that you may stay."

It had taken some persuading, but Karen had been able to convince her father that having an outsider with them for a short period of time would not be harmful. She was sure her father didn't suspect the depths of her interest in John Doe. If he did he would never allow him to stay.

To change the subject, she asked, "How do you like your eggs?"

"Scrambled."

She smiled at him over her shoulder. "Is that a thing you remember?"

"I don't know. It's just the first thing that came to mind."

Using a fork, she whipped the eggs quickly and added them to the skillet. "What is it that you would like to do today?"

"I need to discover why I was in this area."

Wrapping the corner of her apron around the coffeepot handle, she carried it to the table. "If the sheriff could not discover the reason, what makes you think you can?"

He waited until she had finished filling his cup. After taking a sip, he said, "I don't know if I can do better or not, but I have the most at stake. I have to try."

Karen returned the coffeepot to the stove and stirred the eggs. "It seems a simple thing. If you were on this road, then you must have been on your way to, or coming from, one of the farms along this road."

"It's a simple thing if I was on this road in the first place because I wanted to be."

She glanced at him and frowned. "What you mean?"

"The sheriff is going on the assumption that I was robbed and my car was stolen along with my wallet and any personal effects. I could've been dumped here by someone who was attempting to hide my body."

She shook her head. "There are much better places to hide a body than on our farm lane."

"That's exactly what I was thinking."

She dished the eggs onto a plate. After carrying it to the table, she got a second mug, filled it with coffee and sat down across from him. "Will you then visit every farm along this road?"

"That is the only plan I can come up with. What do you think?"

"It makes sense, but it may not be easy." She hesitated not knowing exactly how to phrase her words.

"What do you mean?"

"There are over forty farms along Pleasant View road. Most belong to Amish farmers."

"And?"

"They may not be comfortable talking to an outsider."

Picking up a spoon, he stirred his coffee slowly. After a moment he looked directly into her eyes. "Will you help me?"

She glanced out the window toward the barn.

Papa would not like her getting involved. It troubled her that she was considering helping this man against her father's wishes. But she was.

John must have sensed her reluctance. He said, "If you aren't comfortable with helping me, I understand. You don't know anything about me."

Tipping her head in his direction, she arched one eyebrow. "You don't know much about you, either."

That brought a ghost of a smile to his face. "True."

Crossing her arms on the table she stared at him. "I know that you like scrambled eggs and that you don't want to cause me trouble. I will do what I can to help you, but I am afraid it may not be much."

Rising to her feet, Karen said, "Finish your breakfast. I have much work I must do today, but tomorrow I will drive you to some of our neighbors' farms."

"Are you sure we can't get started today?"

She scowled at him. "Who will bake my bread? Who will mend the clothes my brothers must wear? Who will cook lunch for my father and our evening meal? These things I must do and many more. Tomorrow, I will make time for you. Besides, you need a day of rest. I see it in your eyes."

He looked ready to protest, but finally nodded. "You're right. One more day won't make a difference. You rented me a house, you didn't sign on to be my driver."

"*Goot*, and you will rest, *ja?*"

"I'll try. Does Hope Springs have a public library?"

"Yes. It is across from the English school on Maple Street. Why?"

"I need internet access. There is a national website for missing persons called NamUs. If anyone in the country reports a man of my description missing, the information will be posted there. I know Sheriff Bradley is doing all he can, but he doesn't have much manpower to devote to my case. I must help myself."

"Tomorrow, we can go there first thing."

"No, I'd like to start questioning people first."

"As you wish. Now you must finish your breakfast and get out from under my foot so I may wash the kitchen floor."

He quickly finished his plate, swigged the rest of his coffee and carried everything to the sink. "Is there anything I can do to help?"

"*Ja*. Would you go to the barn and check on *Dat?*"

"Your dad?"

She nodded. "I'm worried about him. He is trying to do too much too soon. He broke his arm five weeks ago when a neighbor's horse kicked him. He wants to get back to work, but the doctor says no. The broken bone damaged a nerve and he has lost feeling in his hand."

"I'll be happy to check on him."

"*Danki.*"

He eyed her intently. "And that means?"

"It means, thank you."

"How do you say, you're welcome?"

"*Du bischt wilkumm.*"

He repeated the phrase and she was surprised by his almost perfect pronunciation. "*Goot.* Now, out, or you will find yourself with a mop in hand."

She was smiling as he walked out, but her grin faded quickly. She had chosen to remain with her family and care for her younger brothers and sisters after their mother was killed. She had given up her chance to marry and have a family of her own because she had been needed here.

At twenty-five, she was considered an old maid by many in the community. She considered herself too old and too wise for a youthful infatuation, but that was exactly the way she felt around John.

He was handsome in his English way, but he was not Plain. So why did a smile on his face make her heart beat faster? It was wrong to think of him in such a way. To forget that would be to bring heartache to all her family. They had suffered enough already. She would not bring them more pain.

Chapter Five

Stepping off the front porch, John looked up. The morning sky hung low, gray and overcast. The wind carried a hint of rain as it scattered fallen leaves across the ground in front of his feet. Glancing over his shoulder, he watched Karen working in the kitchen through the windows. Once again he was struck by how gracefully she moved.

She wore a dark purple dress today with a black apron over it. The color accentuated her willowy frame. The ribbons of her white cap drew his attention to her slender neck, the curve of her jaw and her delicate ears.

He turned away from the sight, recognizing his interest for what it was. The attraction of a man to a lovely woman. He had no business thinking about any woman in a romantic light. Not until he'd solved the riddle of his past.

Heading toward the barn, he studied the looming

structure. It was a huge, solid building, obviously well cared for. Pulling open one of the doors he entered into the dim interior. Instantly, the smells of animals assailed him along with the odors of hay, old wood and feed. He knew these smells the way he knew he was right-handed.

Off to the left was an area that served as Eli's blacksmith shop. Brooms and assorted tools hung from horseshoes attached to the bare wooden walls and overhead beams. Two steel frames suspended from the ceiling had been rigged so they could be released to swing down on either side of a fitful horse during a shoeing. An anvil sat secured to a worn workbench. Beside it was a water barrel and racks of horseshoes of different sizes. A rolling cart in the corner contained all the tools a farrier needed in their proper places.

Walking over to the shoes, John picked one up. It was too heavy. He hefted another. They should be lighter. He didn't know why, but he knew they should be.

The sound of a loud whinny greeted him. He replaced the shoes and moved toward the source. In the filtered daylight he made out a half dozen equine heads hanging over their stall doors to check out this newcomer.

He stopped at the first stall. Molly nuzzled at his shirt pocket. He scratched her head. "Sorry, I didn't know I needed to bring a treat. I'll do better tomorrow."

"Do you like horses, Mr. Doe?"

John turned to see Mr. Imhoff approaching from the back of the barn. In his free hand he held a pitchfork.

"It appears that I do," John answered.

"Is it true what my daughter says? That you have no memory of your life before you were found on our lane?"

"Yes, it's true."

"I have heard of such a thing. My father's oldest brother was kicked in the head by a horse. It was a full day before he recovered his senses."

"I have recovered my senses, just not any personal memories."

"That is a strange burden for God to give a man, but He has His reasons even if we cannot understand them."

Hiding his bitterness at God, John turned back to Molly. "Your mare has nice confirmation. Do you plan to breed her?"

"I've already had two nice colts from her." Eli began walking toward the back of the barn. John followed him to a small paddock where a black horse was trotting back and forth.

John leaned his elbows on the top rail and watched the animal with pleasure. "Hey, pretty boy. You look like you've got some get up and go," he murmured softly.

A blinding pain made him wince. He saw another black horse, rail-thin with its hip bones sticking out. The animal was covered in sores and flies. Death hovered over him.

Sucking in a quick breath, John opened his eyes. The vision was gone.

Eli didn't seem to notice anything unusual. He said, "This one's name is One-Way, and he should look fast. His sire, Willows Way, won the Hamiltonian at the Meadowlands ten years ago."

John rubbed the ache from his temple. "I'm sorry, I'm afraid that doesn't mean anything to me."

"It means his sire was a racehorse, a trotter and a *goot* one."

John looked at the Amish farmer in his dark coat, long gray beard and worn black hat. "You are raising racehorses?"

Eli smiled. "Mostly I raise and train carriage horses. I bought my first Standardbred when I was a teenager. I was looking for a fast horse to impress my girlfriend."

"How did that work out?"

"The courtship did not, but the horse did. I got interested in the breed, began to study trade magazines and it wasn't long before I was breeding them myself. Back then I couldn't afford the stud fees of high-profile stallions. I got very *goot* at losing money at what my wife called my foolishness."

"Isn't horse racing and betting against your religion?"

"*Ja*, it is a worldly thing and thus forbidden to us."

"Okay, then I'm confused."

Eli's grin widened. "There is nothing wrong in breeding a fine horse. They are God's creatures, after all. If you can sell that horse for an honest price, there is nothing wrong with that, either. This one's brother is doing well on the racing circuit this year."

John smiled as understanding dawned. "I see. If the fine horse should win a race or two for some new owner, then the next foal from your mare will be worth even more money."

"*Ja*. It is all in the hands of God. I try to remember to keep Him first in my life for He rewards His faithful servants."

"When will you sell this fellow?"

"After the first of the year I will take him to the Winter Speed sale in Delaware, Ohio."

The place meant nothing to John.

Eli said, "My daughter has taken a keen interest in you."

John was surprised by the abrupt change of topic. "Your daughter has been very kind."

"She has a *goot* heart. It was the same with her mother." Eli's voice became wistful.

"I'm sorry for your loss. Karen told me what happened."

Eli turned to John. In a low steely voice, he said, "I would not want to see my daughter's kindness repaid with sorrow. Be careful of that, John Doe."

Taken aback, John stared at Eli. The last thing he wanted was to cause trouble for the woman who'd shown him so much kindness. He nodded solemnly. "I will, sir. I promise."

Late the following morning, Karen stopped the buggy where the lane met the highway and gave a sidelong glance at John seated beside her. He turned the collar of his coat up against the cold drizzle, but his excitement at finally getting to do something shimmered in his eyes.

"Which way would you like to go?" she asked.

"Which direction is the nearest interstate?"

She pointed north. "If you go through town and then take Yoder Road north about twenty-five miles you will reach the interstate."

"Let's go toward Hope Springs then and stop at the farms between here and the town. If I'm not from the area I most likely came in on a major highway."

Slapping the reins against Molly's rump, Karen sent the mare trotting down the blacktop. "I have one stop I need to make at the Sutters' farm. Are you certain you are not from this area?"

"No. Except that no one has reported me missing from around here. And no one has recognized me from the TV piece the local news ran on me. Do you mind if I try my hand at driving?" he asked.

Surprised by his request, she said, "*Nee,* I do not mind. Do you know how to drive a horse?"

"I think I can. I've been watching you do it." Taking the reins, he sat up straight and guided Molly down the highway.

After watching for a few minutes, Karen said, "That is *goot.* I think you've done this before."

John smiled at her. "I think you're right."

"Perhaps you are ex-Amish."

The moment the words left her mouth her heart sank like a stone. If John had taken the vows of their faith and then left the community, all would shun him. She would have to shun him.

He didn't seem to notice her concern. "The sheriff did discuss that possibility."

Dismissing the idea as unacceptable, she said, "You don't speak or understand our language. Surely you could not forget the tongue you grew up with."

He shrugged. "Who would think I could forget

my own name? As far as I'm concerned anything is possible."

Racking her mind for local families with members who'd strayed, she quickly came up with several. In their tight-knit community, she was sure she knew all the young men who'd left. The only one close to John's age would have been Isaac Troyer's son who left almost ten years ago. He looked nothing like John. The others she could think of who had left the community were much younger men and a few young women.

There were at least three families who had moved into the area recently. If they had members leave the faith before coming to this church district she didn't know about them.

In less than a quarter of a mile, they reached the lane of another farm. John turned the horse onto the narrow road. Karen said, "When we get to the bishop's house, you should stay in the buggy."

"Why?"

"So that I may speak privately to Bishop Zook and ask if he can assist you."

"And if he says no?" John's tone carried a hint of annoyance.

"Bishop Zook is a wise and much-respected man. If you have his permission to speak to the members of our church it will open many doors that might otherwise be closed to you."

John relented. "All right. I'll follow your lead."

"Goot." She nodded her satisfaction.

Driving the buggy up to the front of the house, he drew the mare to a stop. Before Karen could step out, Joseph Zook walked out of the house toward her.

"Guder mariye, Karen," he called cheerfully. "What brings you here today?"

"Good morning, Bishop. I have brought someone to meet you. This is John Doe, the man who was found unconscious beside our lane."

Concern furrowed the minister's brow. "I have heard the story. I am glad to see that you are recovered, Mr. Doe."

"I'm not quite recovered, sir." John touched the bandage on the side of his head. "I have no memory of my past. I'm hoping that you can help me."

"I am sorry for your injury, but how can I help?"

"Do you recognize me? Have you ever seen me before?"

The bishop studied him intently then said, *"Nee,* I have not."

Karen could feel John's disappointment in the slump of his body beside her. She addressed the bishop. "John wishes to speak to members of our church to see if anyone knows him or knows something about him."

The bishop studied Karen intently. He switched

to Pennsylvania Dutch. "You must be careful, Karen. To become involved in this outsider business is not a good thing."

She bowed her head slightly. "How can helping an injured man be a bad thing? I feel that this is what God wants me to do."

"Be sure it is God's will you are seeking, Karen, and not your own."

"I will heed your advice, Bishop."

The bishop turned his attention back to John and spoke in English. "You may speak to members of our church if they wish it also. I will pray that you find the answers you seek, young man."

Karen watched the bishop walk away. She had been warned. Her support for John must be limited and above reproach. She reached for the reins but John ignored her outstretched hand, turning the horse easily in the yard and sending her down the lane.

Karen put the bishop's warning behind her. "You have driven a buggy many times."

"Maybe I'm just a fast learner."

"Perhaps." Her spirits sank lower. How many English knew how to drive a buggy? Not many. It seemed more likely that her earlier assumption was correct. John had been raised Plain.

If he had left the church before his baptism, he would be accepted by most of the Amish in her community. If, on the other hand, he had rejected the church after baptism he would be considered an outcast until he made a full confession before the congregation.

She glanced at him once more. How could a man confess his sins if he had no memory of them? He looked happy at the moment driving Molly along at a steady pace. The cold rain had stopped and the sun peeked out. Up ahead on the road, Henry Zook, the bishop's youngest son, was traveling to market in his farm wagon. John slowed Molly to follow behind him. When the way was clear and free of traffic, he sent Molly high stepping around the wagon.

When the mare drew level with the other horses she suddenly picked up her pace eager to get in front of them.

"You've got some speed, Molly girl," John called to the horse.

Instead of letting the mare keep her fast pace, he reined her in and grinned at Karen. "I'd love to let her go and see just how much she's got."

"Why don't you?" she asked, hoping to hear the right answer.

He shook his head. "No, she has too many miles to haul us yet. It wouldn't be kind to wear her out on a joyride."

Looking straight ahead, Karen smiled inwardly. "Whatever you have done in your past life, you care about animals. You can add it to your list of things you have discovered about yourself."

"Now if I can only locate a pencil sharpener," he added drily.

"What?" She tipped her head to stare at him in confusion.

"Never mind. Where to next?"

"Up ahead is the farm of Elam Sutter. He and some of his family moved here from Pennsylvania almost two years ago. Elam is getting married next week."

Twisting in the seat, she grasped his arm as excitement rippled though her mind. "I don't know why I didn't think of it sooner. It makes perfect sense."

"What makes perfect sense?"

"Perhaps you were coming for the wedding. Elam's fiancée, Katie Lantz, lived out in the world for several years. She knows many English. That must be it."

John tried not to get his hopes up but Karen's excitement was contagious. He asked, "Why didn't they report me as missing?"

"I don't know. Maybe they weren't sure when you would arrive. Maybe your coming was a surprise for them."

He wanted to believe her scenarios but he was

growing used to disappointment. Still, his palms began to sweat. "We will see soon enough."

As they rolled into the yard, John saw four other buggies lined up beside the barn. He drew Molly to stop in front of the house.

Karen withdrew a large box from the back of the buggy. John took it from her and followed her to the front door. He was surprised when she didn't knock but went right in. The spacious kitchen was filled to overflowing with enticing smells of baking and the happy chatter of a half dozen women engaged in cleaning and polishing every surface in the house.

The oldest woman in the room came forward drying her hands on her white apron. With a bright smile on her face, she said, "Karen, how nice to see you."

Karen said, "I've brought some of my mother's best bowls and platters for you to use at the wedding, Nettie."

"Wonderful. They will come in handy. I've forgotten how much work it takes to get ready for a wedding dinner." Nettie indicated a place for John to set his burden.

Karen said, "I have come with another errand, Nettie. Everyone, this is John Doe, the man who was found injured on our farm." Karen smiled encouragement at him.

The room grew quiet. John felt everyone's eyes

on him. He scanned their faces looking for any hint of recognition. He saw nothing but blank stares. Either they had no idea who he was, or they were very good actresses. Once again his hopes slipped away. Why didn't someone know him? Why?

Looking over the group, Karen asked, "Where is Katie?"

Nettie said, "She is upstairs changing the baby."

One of the other women stepped forward. "Are you a friend of Katie's? I am Ruby, her future sister-in-law. This is my sister Mary, my sister-in-law Sally Yoder, and this is my mother, Nettie Sutter."

John nodded to them. "I'm not sure if I know Katie. I sure hope she knows me. The injury to my head robbed me of my memory. Karen thinks I may have been coming to the wedding."

Ruby and Mary exchanged puzzled glances. The two women were in their late twenties or early thirties. They were clearly related to Nettie. The women shared the same bright blue eyes, apple-red cheeks and blond hair although Nettie's was streaked with silver. They all wore plain dresses with white caps and white aprons.

The teenager, Sally, had red hair and freckles, but she wasn't smiling in welcome the way the others were. Her eyes held a frightened, guarded look. She said, "I will go get Katie."

Spinning around, she opened a door and rushed up the stairs beyond.

He waited, not taking his eyes off the stairwell. After an eternity, he heard footsteps coming down. The woman who entered the kitchen was dressed in the same Amish fashion as the others, but her hair was black as coal. She came toward him with a perplexed expression in her dark eyes. He held his breath, not daring to hope.

Stopping in front of him, she said, "Emma Wadler mentioned that she had met you at the inn, Mr. Doe. I'm sorry I can't be of any help. I don't recognize you."

He could barely swallow past the lump in his throat. A vicious headache, brought on by his frustration, sapped his strength. He managed to say, "I'm sorry we interrupted your afternoon. Thank you for your time."

Nettie spoke up, "Would you like some tea? I have the kettle on."

He shook his head, eager to escape before the pounding in his temple made him sick.

Katie said, "Elam is in his workshop. Perhaps he has met you before."

After looking at John closely, Karen said, "Come with me. I will show you the way."

He followed her outside into the fresh, cool air.

Only then did he realize how hot the kitchen had been. Breathing deeply, he struggled to master the pain in his head.

"Take slow deep breaths," Karen said, standing at his side.

"I'm okay. How did you know?" If he kept his eyes closed the pain wasn't as bad.

"My mother used to get migraines. Do they happen to you often?" she asked gently.

"Two or three times since I woke up in the hospital."

She led him toward a small bench set beneath the bare gnarled branches of an apple tree. "Sit here. I will fetch Elam."

John was in no shape to argue. Leaning back against the rough bark of the tree, he let his mind go blank. Slowly, the pain receded.

"Hey, buddy, think fast."

John's eyes popped open as he threw up his hands to catch the apple being thrown at him. Only there was none. He was alone. He closed his eyes again and rebuilt the scene in his mind.

The tree overhead was lush with green leaves and heavy with fruit. Yellow apples. He was sitting on the cool grass with his back against the trunk of the tree. A hot breeze flowed over his skin, making him glad of the shade. Birds were singing nearby. An occasional raucous cry sounded from among them. He heard the drone of insects, then the pad of footsteps approaching.

Close by, a woman's voice, low and sweet said, "Here is my geils-mann *loafing under a tree."*

He tried to turn his head to see her face, but found himself staring at his boots, instead. The harder he tried to see her, the more rapidly the scene faded.

"John? John, this is Elam Sutter."

Opening his eyes, John saw Karen standing in front of him. Blinking hard, he looked around. The tree branches were bare. The lawn was brown and curled in winter sleep. Behind Karen, a tall, broad-shouldered man in a dark coat and black Amish hat stood regarding him intently.

Sharp bitterness lanced through John at the loss of his brief summer memory. His identity had been so close he could almost touch it and now it was gone.

How often could his mind be torn in two this way without finally ripping into pieces?

Chapter Six

Disappointment drained John's strength. The memory was gone. He couldn't get it back, but Karen and her friend were still waiting for him to speak.

He forced himself to rise and extended his hand to Elam. "I'm pleased to meet you, Mr. Sutter. I guess Karen has told you why I'm here."

Elam's grip was strong and firm. "She has. I do not know your face, John Doe. I wish I could be more help."

"Thank you. I'm sorry we interrupted your work."

The sound of the front door closing made them all look toward the house. Katie came out wrapping a black shawl around her shoulders. John happened to glance at Elam's face. The soft smile and the glow in the Amishman's eyes told John this was a love match. When Katie reached them,

Elam slipped an arm around her waist to block the cold.

She said to John, "Are you sure you won't come in for a while? We have hot apple pie and coffee if you'd like."

"No, but thank you. Congratulations on your engagement."

"*Danki,*" Katie blushed sweetly as she gazed at Elam with adoring eyes. John wondered if a woman had ever looked at him that way.

After bidding the couple farewell, John followed Karen to the buggy. He relinquished the reins to her, knowing his headache wouldn't let him keep his mind on the road. They were getting ready to leave when Nettie came racing out of the house carrying a large basket covered with a checkered cloth.

Breathlessly, she reached them and handed the basket to Karen. "This is for you and your family. A couple of my peach pies because I know Eli likes them best. How is he doing?"

Karen accepted the basket. "He gets his cast off next week, but he must still wear a brace and sling. He is chaffing at the bit to get back to work."

"Has feeling returned to his hand?"

"Some, but he has no strength in it."

"The poor man. He's coming to the wedding, isn't he?" A faint crease of worry appeared between Nettie's brows.

"He would not miss it," Karen assured her.

Relief smoothed away Nettie's frown. "That is *goot*. And you, Mr. Doe, you are welcome to come to the wedding dinner. There will be plenty of food and there will be other English there, too," she added with a bright smile.

"Thank you. That is very kind." He tried to be noncommittal. Attending the wedding of someone he barely knew seemed presumptuous.

Nettie fixed her gaze on Karen. "Tell your father…tell him I think about him often. When this wedding fuss is over you must all come for Sunday dinner."

"We will look forward to it."

John closed his eyes and rubbed his brow as Karen drove Molly back to the highway. The jolting and creaking of the buggy added nausea to his discomfort.

Karen pulled Molly to a halt when they reached the end of the Sutters' lane. "Do you still wish to go into Hope Springs?"

What he wanted was to lie down somewhere dark and quiet and let his mind travel back to that green, hot place and stay there until he saw the face of the woman who had been with him. As much as he wanted to do that, he knew he couldn't stop now. "Let's keep going. I want to see as many people as I can today."

* * *

Karen studied John with deep concern. His color was pale, his eyes sunken with pain. He looked as if he might topple out of the buggy at any second. He kept one hand pressed to his forehead in an attempt to block the light from his eyes.

When she didn't start Molly moving, he glanced at her. "What's wrong? I said let's go into town."

She let out a sigh. "*Nee*, we are going home. You have done too much today. You are in pain and you need rest."

He sat up straight to hide his weakness. "I'm fine. It's just a headache."

"Men! Always trying to show how tough they are. Anyone with eyes in their head can see you are done in. We will go home now and that is the end of it. Tomorrow will be here soon enough."

"I'll be okay," he insisted.

"*Ja.* When you have had a rest I'm sure you will be fine." Clicking her tongue, she urged Molly onto the highway and sent her trotting briskly toward their farm.

"Are you always this domineering?"

He had no idea how tough she could be, but he just might find out. "When I must tell a child what to do, *ja*, I am."

"Now you're saying I'm acting like a child?"

"A stubborn, willful child."

"I'm going to let that slide. I can see arguing with you is fruitless. When did you take over the job of raising your brothers and sister?"

"I am the eldest daughter. It is expected of me to care for the younger ones. My mother was killed four years ago if that is what you are asking?"

"You do a good job with them."

"They are *goot* children. They make the job easy."

"Even Jacob?"

"Jacob is in a hurry to be the man of the house. He wants to take over for our father until Papa is well."

"But you don't want him to do that."

She hadn't realized her fear was that transparent. "Being a farrier is a hard job. It takes strength. A man must know how to read a horse. Some of the draft horses my father works on weigh nearly a ton. A man can shoe a horse nine times without trouble and on the tenth time that horse decides he wants to kill the farrier."

"I didn't say you were wrong to worry."

Her annoyance slipped away. "I'm sorry. It's just that he is so young yet. He idolized Seth, our brother who was killed. Seth was big and strong like Papa, not slender like Jacob. Seth had the touch when it came to horses. Mamm used to say he could whisper to them and they did just as he wished. Jacob wants to be a horseman like Seth was but he is impatient."

John sat back and stared into space. "A horseman. He wants to be a horseman, a *geils-mann*. Here is my *geils-mann* loafing under a tree."

Karen eyed him with concern. "What are you talking about?"

He focused on her face. "I had another memory flash. It was summer, and I was sitting under an apple tree. There was a woman behind me. She said, 'Here is my *geils-mann* loafing under a tree.' I heard the words clear as day."

"Who was she?" Karen asked.

"I don't know. I didn't see her face."

"How did you know what the word meant?" she asked in surprise.

"I'm not sure. I just know."

As the ramifications of his comment sank in, Karen's heart sank, too. *Geils-mann* was an Amish expression. Only someone raised speaking Pennsylvania Dutch would use the word. If John had not been raised Amish then the woman he spoke of surely had been. Karen glanced at John. Who was John Doe and who was this woman to him?

Several days later, John was outside early in the morning gathering a load of wood for his stove when he saw Nick Bradley drive into the yard.

John's heart jumped into overdrive. Maybe the sheriff's investigation had turned up something new. He waited with bated breath as Nick climbed out of his SUV.

Touching the brim of his hat, Nick said, "Morning. I was in the neighborhood and thought I'd check and see how you're doing."

"I'm fine. Have you learned anything new?"

"No. I'm sorry."

John's anticipation drained away. He carried the logs to the box beside his front door and dropped them. He'd have to learn not to get his hopes up. Somehow.

Nick said, "I was hoping you might have found out something. Not that I want you to make me look bad."

"No worries. I'm still a walking blank. I've had a few flashes of memory, but nothing concrete."

"Are you writing them down?"

John paused and looked at the sheriff. "I hadn't thought of that."

"You should. Even the smallest thing you recall might help me. How's the head?" He pointed to John's bandage.

"Better."

"My cousin Amber wanted me to remind you that you need to come in to Dr. White's office and get your stitches out."

He rubbed gingerly at his dressing. The sutures

had started to itch. "I know I was supposed to go in a few days ago, but I've had other things on my mind."

"I've got time to run you into Hope Springs this morning. Shall I see if they can work you in? I'm free for a while unless I get a call."

"That would be great, but how do I get back if you've got to leave?" A light dusting of snow covered the ground this morning and occasional flakes drifted down from the gray sky. John didn't want to walk five miles back to the farm in this weather.

"We have a couple of folks in town that provide taxi services to the Amish. Amber can arrange a ride if you need it." Nick made the phone call.

After a brief conversation, he closed the phone. "All set. They can see you in half an hour."

"Let me tell Miss Imhoff where I'm going. She likes to keep a tight leash on me."

Nick chuckled. "I've heard she can be a tough cookie."

The two men walked toward the main house. Nick asked, "How's it working out? You staying here."

"It's fine. The boy, Jacob, isn't thrilled, but Noah and Anna don't seem to mind. Eli is taking a wait-and-see attitude."

"And Karen?"

John glanced toward the house. "She's been very kind."

Before they reached the steps, Eli came out to greet them. His stoic face showed nothing of what he was thinking. He nodded to the sheriff. "*Goot* day to you."

"The same to you, Eli. I'm going to take John into town so Doc White can check him out. I'll see that he gets back, too. How is your arm?"

Flexing his fingers in the sling, Eli said, "It is healing."

Jacob came out of the house followed by Anna and Noah. The children hung back at the sight of the sheriff.

Nick glanced from Eli to Jacob. "I had a complaint about some Amish boys racing buggies over on Sky Road yesterday. You wouldn't know anything about that, would you?"

"*Nee.* We do not," Eli stated firmly. John caught the furtive glance Jacob shot in the sheriff's direction before looking down.

Nick nodded. "It's dangerous business racing on a public road. Gina Curtis had to put her car in the ditch to avoid hitting someone. It did a fair amount of damage to her front end. None of the buggy drivers stuck around. She wasn't hurt but she could have been."

Eli glanced at his son. "Do you know anything about this?"

"No, Papa." Jacob glared at the sheriff. If he did know something, he wasn't talking. Noah remained uncharacteristically quiet.

Eli said, "Go on to school now, children."

The kids rushed down the steps with their lunch pails in hand and headed toward the school two miles away. Several times they threw looks over their shoulders. John had the distinct feeling they did know something.

After bidding Mr. Imhoff goodbye, John climbed in the sheriff's SUV. When Nick got in and started the truck, John said, "You think Jacob was involved, don't you?"

Nick turned the vehicle around and drove out the lane. They passed the children walking. Only Anna waved.

Nick said, "Gina's description could fit ten boys in this area. I didn't expect to get a confession. Illicit buggy racing goes on amongst Amish teenagers the same way drag racing goes on among the English kids. A lot of Amish parents turn a blind eye to that kind of behavior during the *rumspringa*."

"What's that?"

"It means running-around years. Amish teens are free to experiment with things that won't be allowed once they join the church. You'll see their buggies outfitted with boom boxes, they'll have cell phones and they'll dress like regular kids when they are away from the farm. Jacob is young for that type of behavior. *Rumspringa* normally starts when the kids are about sixteen, but his dad has some fine horses."

"Yes, he does."

The sheriff looked at him sharply. "Do you know something about horses?"

"I know which end is which. I seem to know what a good Standardbred looks like. I found out I can drive a buggy and Eli's two-wheeled cart without a problem. He's been letting me use the cart to visit farms around here. The one thing I did remember was a woman's voice. She called me her *geils-mann*."

"She called you her horseman? That's interesting. Maybe we ruled out your being ex-Amish too soon. It's good to hear things are coming back to you."

John had been wondering about the young woman ever since his vision. Was she his sister, a friend, his wife? He had no way of knowing.

He turned to stare out the window. "Not enough things are coming back to me."

Karen didn't want to reveal to her father her burning curiosity about the sheriff's visit. Instead, when he came inside, she served him another cup of coffee before casually asking, "Where is the sheriff taking John?"

"To see the doctor in town."

"Oh." Relief made her knees weak. He wasn't taking him away to his old life. She sat down quickly. Even though that was what she prayed for, losing him, even for the right reason, wasn't something she wanted to face. Not yet.

Eli watched her closely. "You have taken a great liking to John Doe."

Apparently her feelings weren't as well hidden as she had hoped. She toyed with the corner of her apron. "He is so lost. I wish to help him. That is all."

Her father covered her hands with his own. "Take care, daughter. He is not one of us."

"He is one of God's children."

"Do not seek to divert me. You know exactly what I mean. Our faith makes no exceptions for those who stray outside the *Ordnung*."

"I have done nothing against the rules of the church. John will only be here a few more days." She forced herself to smile in reassurance, but her father was not fooled.

"I should have encouraged you to marry long ago, but I was so befuddled without your mother. It was selfish of me."

"Papa, I am happy caring for the little ones and keeping your house. I could not ask for more."

Sadness filled his eyes. "I would ask for more in your life. A woman should have a husband to love and shelter her. The risk of temptation would not be so great."

Karen looked down at her hands. "I am not tempted by John Doe."

"Do not forget that I am a man like all other men. I see the way he looks at you. I see the way you try not to look back at him."

She pulled her hands away from his. "I care about him. I don't deny that. When I saw him lying on the ground bleeding and wounded, I saw Seth. I could not save my brother. He died in my arms. I know his death was the will of God. Just as I know John lived by the will of God alone."

"We do not know why God brings sadness or joy into our lives. We only know all comes from His purpose for us." Eli leaned back in his chair and took a sip of coffee.

"I know that, Papa. But why has God taken away John's memory? I believe it is because God wants to show John something he could not see before."

Eli grasped her hand again. "Karen, Karen, you cannot know this. You cannot presume to know *Gotte wille*."

She looked into his eyes so full of concern. "I'm sorry, Papa. I did not mean to upset you. Please trust me when I say you have nothing to worry about."

Leaning forward, she said earnestly, "My heart

is here, with you, and with the children. Nothing could make me throw that away."

He relaxed and nodded slightly. "You have always been a *goot* daughter and strong in your faith. You see something in the *Englischer* that I do not see. You may be right. God sent John Doe into our midst for a reason. I will keep an open mind about this man."

John entered the Hope Springs Medical Clinic, a modern one-story blond brick building, with a niggling sense of dread. He'd had enough of hospitals and doctors without getting any answers in return. Inside, he checked in with the elderly receptionist and took a seat in the waiting room. He didn't have to wait long.

A young woman in a white lab coat and blue scrubs called his name. He followed her down a short hallway and took a seat on the exam-room table.

"It's nice to finally meet you, Mr. Doe. I'm Amber Bradley, Nick Bradley's cousin." She stuck a thermometer under John's tongue.

She removed it when it beeped and John said, "You're the one I need to thank for the financial help."

Wrapping a blood-pressure cuff around his arm, she said, "You're welcome, but it wasn't just me. A lot of people wanted to help."

John remained quiet until she had finished with his blood pressure. When she took the stethoscope out of her ears, he said, "I wasn't aware that I required a midwife."

She chuckled. "I am a woman with many hats. One of those being an office nurse."

The door opened and a tall, distinguished man with silver hair came in leaning heavily on a cane. "Yes, and she is proof that good help is hard to come by these days."

"Ha!" she retorted. "You just try running this office without me, Harold."

"No doubt I'll have to when you marry what's-his-name," he grumbled.

"Is that any way to talk about your grandson? Don't worry, Mr. Doe, Dr. White's bark is worse than his bite." She checked John's ears, his eyes and then his throat.

Dr. White, who had been reading John's chart, said, "You are a very interesting case, Mr. Doe."

"So I've been told." John tried not to let his bitterness show. He hated being an oddity, the freak with a damaged mind.

"I imagine you're tired of hearing that." The doctor washed his hands and pulled on a pair of latex gloves.

"Good guess."

Harold began removing the bandage from John's head. "We medical people live for cases like yours. The odd thing, the unusual diagnoses. It's like catnip to us. We want to define it, study it, understand it, cure it."

John winced as the tape pulled his hair. "I'm in favor of a cure. Tell me which pill to take."

"Amnesia following a trauma isn't unusual, but normally it involves losing a short period of time just prior to the injury. A prolonged and complete amnesia such as you have is exceedingly rare."

"Lucky me." This time John didn't disguise his sarcasm.

"Your scalp is healed nicely. How are your ribs?"

"Not bad if I take it slow."

"Good. I'm going to have Amber take out the stitches. Any headaches?"

"Sometimes."

"Bad ones?"

"They can be. I think they're getting better. Maybe I'm just getting used to them."

"Is there any particular thing that triggers them?" The doctor pulled off his gloves and picked up John's chart.

"I get these flashes, like images from a movie. I think they are memories, but I can't be sure. When that happens the pain gets intense."

"You say you think they're memories. Anything specific?"

John felt stupid sharing the few instances that

he'd had. "Frying trout. A woman laughing. A sick or starving horse. A woman using an Amish word. Nothing with any context of time or place."

"The same woman?" Amber asked.

"I'm not sure. I don't see her face."

"Are these flashes becoming more frequent?" The doctor made a note on the chart.

John held still as Amber began removing his stitches. "Not that I can tell. Some days I'll have one or two, some days I won't have any."

He winced but didn't yelp as she worked on one stubborn stitch. Finally, she said, "All done. You'll just need to keep it clean and dry, but otherwise you're good to go. I understand you're staying at Eli Imhoff's place."

"Yes. That's where I was found. I've been interviewing the Amish in the area for the past several days hoping to find someone who recognizes me. I mean, I must have been in the area for a reason."

Closing the chart, Dr. White asked, "You've been going door-to-door?"

"I started with the farms closest to where I was found but I'm not having much luck. Don't get me wrong. The Amish have been forthcoming, maybe because I've had Karen Imhoff with me, but no one knows anything."

Amber and Dr. White exchanged glances. Amber said, "There might be an easier way to meet people than going to every house in the area."

John looked at her with interest. "How?"

Dr. White said, "November is the month for Amish weddings. Sometimes as many as four hundred people show up for them. Elam Sutter's wedding is this coming Thursday."

"Nettie Sutter did invite me to the supper."

"Great," Amber said, looking at Harold. "Phillip and I will be there, too."

"Oh, and I'm chopped liver now?" Harold asked, a teasing edge in his tone.

Amber smiled at John. "Dr. Harold White will also be attending the event, and he knows every soul in this county."

Harold met John's gaze and said, "Chances are almost everyone there will have already heard your story."

"How?" John asked. "They don't have radio or TV."

Amber laughed. "You would be surprised how fast news travels in a small community like this."

Harold rubbed his chin. "I'm sure the Imhoff family will be going for the entire day. Why don't you ride along with me, young man? I'll introduce you around and see if we can come up with someone who knows you."

John realized it could be his best chance to

meet many of the reclusive Amish in the area. He inclined his head. "Sir, I would be delighted to accompany you."

Chapter Seven

True to his word, Nick stuck around to give John a lift from the clinic back to the farm. As the sheriff drove away, John stood in the yard staring at the farmhouse. Once again he was struck by how tidy the farmstead was. The fences were all in good repair, the barn and outbuildings had been recently painted. Everything spoke of order and neatness. Eli Imhoff was a good steward of his land.

Shoving his hands in his pockets, John wondered what kind of steward he was. Did he have lands and a home to care for? Or did he live in an apartment in a crowded city? If he could wish for a home—it would be one like this.

Instead of going into the grandfather house, John made his way to the barn and to the stalls where the horses stood dozing or munching grain. He was surprised by how comfortable he felt among them. Sometime in his life he must've worked on a ranch or farm. If only he could remember where or when.

He was petting the nose of the big draft horse when he heard a door open. Looking over his shoulder, he saw Karen coming from another part of the barn. In her hands she carried a pail brimming full of apples.

Her face brightened when she caught sight of him. "You are back. What did the doctor say?"

John moved to take the pail from her. "He said I'm doing good. Except for not remembering anything, of course."

"You will remember when God wills it."

"I wish He'd hurry up, I'm tired of living in the dark."

"I know it is a terrible burden for you."

"You must be tired of hearing me complain. What are the apples for?"

"I'm putting up applesauce."

"Need some help?"

She slanted a grin at him. "Can you pare an apple?"

Giving an exaggerated shrug, he said, "Only one way to find out."

Inside the house, John sat at the kitchen table and quickly discovered he could use a paring knife. As he cored and chopped the contents of the bucket into a large bowl he had a chance to observe Karen at work.

Every move she made was efficient. She seemed to know exactly what she needed to do when she needed to do it. The canning jars were washed and placed in a large kettle and boiled. Setting them aside after ten minutes, she put his chopped apples into a second kettle. Before long the mouthwatering aroma of cooking apples and cinnamon filled the air.

"I hope you're not going to can all of it," he said as he started cutting the last pile of apples. His stomach rumbled loudly.

She wiped her brow with the back of her hand. The steam had given her face a rosy glow. "I am saving plenty for supper."

He tipped his head. "I think I should have a taste now in case the apples were bad. You don't want to give bad applesauce to your family."

She fisted her hands on her hips. "Of all the pieces you sampled while you were chopping, how many were sour?"

"Okay, I'm busted. I missed lunch, you know. Do you have eyes in the back of your head under that bonnet thing?"

"I don't need eyes in the back of my head. I brought in enough apples to make eight pints. I can see I'm only going to have enough to fill seven jars."

"If I promise to go get more fruit can I have a dish of those apples before you squish them?"

Karen laughed and pulled a brown ceramic bowl from the cupboard. "*Ja,* but you had better not complain if it spoils your supper."

As she heaped the bowl full of stewed apples, John quickly carved an apple skin into the shape of huge red lips and stuck it between his teeth. When Karen turned around and saw him she doubled over with laughter, nearly spilling his snack on the floor. For the first time in his new life John felt totally happy.

Later that evening, when everyone was finishing their meal, he caught Karen's eye, wiggled his brows and held up his empty plate with a wide grin. She smothered an abrupt giggle, causing her family members to stare at her. Rising quickly, she began to clear the table.

John said, "Let me help you."

Anna, also in the process of gathering up plates, gave him a funny look. "This is woman's work." She looked at her father for confirmation. "Isn't it, Papa?"

Eli glanced at Karen and then at his boys. "A man must know how to do a woman's work if his wife needs help just as a woman must know how to do a man's work if her husband needs help."

Noah eyed the dirty dishes in disgust. "But you don't need help tonight, do you Karen?"

"*Nee,* Anna and I can manage, but thank you for your offer."

John slipped his hands in the front pockets of his jeans wishing he could spend more time with Karen but knowing it wasn't wise.

Noah said, "Come and play checkers with me, John."

Relieved, John followed the boy into the living room where Noah quickly set up the board. Eli settled himself in his favorite chair, opened his Bible and began reading. Jacob pretended interest in a book of his own, but his eyes were drawn repeatedly to the game.

Karen and Anna joined the men when they were done in the kitchen. Karen pulled a basket of mending from the cupboard in the corner, sat down beside her father and began to thread a needle. It seemed to John that she was never idle. Anna brought out a small, faceless doll to play with.

John's gaze was drawn repeatedly to where Karen sat. The lamplight gave a soft glow to her face. A gentle smile curved her lips. The white bonnet on her hair reminded him of a halo.

She was so beautiful it hurt his eyes, and he had no business admiring her.

"Your move," Noah said.

John realized he'd been staring and focused his attention on his play.

Anna came to John's elbow. "Do you want to hear the poem I'm going to recite for the school Christmas program?"

Noah shook his head. "Not again. We've heard it a million times."

"Noah, she needs the practice," Karen chided gently.

John said, "I haven't heard it. Miss Anna, I would love to hear your poem."

Flashing him a bright smile, she folded her hands and stared at a spot over his head. *"Auf einer Nacht so ehrlich in einem Land weit entfernt."*

Jacob snickered. "He doesn't understand German, Anna."

She propped her hands on her hips. "David Yoder is repeating it in English at the program so everyone will know what it means."

John sought to soothe her. "You say it just as you will at your program. When you're done, you can interpret it for me."

Her smile returned. "The first line means on a night so fair in a land far away."

"Got it. Let me hear the whole thing. I'm sure Noah will tell me if you mess up."

Noah chuckled. "You know that's right."

Anna began again. As she spoke, John caught Karen's eye. The look she gave him conveyed her approval. A warm feeling of happiness settled over him. He smiled back at her.

Eli cleared his throat. John caught the stern look he shot his daughter. Karen quickly returned to her sewing. John gave his attention back to the checkerboard.

After Anna finished her poem she went back to playing with her doll. When Noah lost his third match in a row to John, he dropped his head onto his forearms. "Jacob always wins, too."

John ruffled the boy's hair. "You almost had me on that last one."

Eli closed his Bible. "Do you play chess, Mr. Doe?"

Did he? John tried to see the pieces and the moves in his mind. He nodded. "I think so."

"Jacob has a talent for the game. Why don't you two play?"

"I'm willing." John looked at the boy. Indecision flashed across Jacob's face.

Not wanting to push the kid, John began clearing the checkers from the board. He hummed a tune softly as he stacked them inside the box. When the board was clear, he looked at Jacob. The boy's face had gone pale. He snapped his book shut. "I'm going to bed."

John watched Jacob rush out of the room and wondered what he had done to upset the youngster. He looked at Karen. She just shrugged her shoulders.

Folding up the chessboard, John handed it to

Noah. Rising to his feet, he said, "I think I'll turn in, too."

Laying her mending aside, Karen said, "I will get you a lamp. It is dark out."

In the kitchen, she pulled a kerosene lamp from a cabinet. Setting it on the counter, she lifted the glass chimney and lit the wick.

John took it from her hand. "I'm sorry if I've upset your family. Maybe my staying here wasn't a good idea."

"It is only for a couple more days. We can manage."

Gazing into her luminous eyes, John found himself wishing he could stay longer. The thought was foolish and he knew it.

Once he found out about his past, then maybe he could start thinking about a future. Until then he would be crazy to get attached to anyone, especially the lovely Amish woman standing before him.

The beautiful autumn morning of the wedding dawned cold but clear. After making sure everyone in the family was dressed in their Sunday best Karen ushered them out to the waiting buggy. Jacob had gone ahead with the bench wagon. The special enclosed wagon held the several dozen narrow wooden benches that their church district used for Sunday services.

Karen glanced toward the *dawdy haus* and saw John watching them from the porch. For the past several days he'd been making himself at home on the farm, helping her father with the horses and her with chores. Having him across from her at the supper table had become the high point of her evenings. But he would be moving to the inn tomorrow. His time with her family was almost up. There wouldn't be any more afternoons spent laughing over a pail of apples.

He lifted a hand in a brief wave. Karen glanced at her father and saw he was watching her. She didn't wave back but climbed in the buggy instead.

The trip into town was accomplished in short order. The wedding ceremony itself was to take place at the home of Naomi and Emma Wadler, both friends of the bride. When Karen and her family entered the house the bridal party was already sitting in the front row of the wooden benches.

Katie wore a new plain dress of light blue. Elam looked quite handsome in his dark coat and not the least bit nervous. Near them sat two each of Elam's sisters and brothers-in-law, their wedding attendants.

Nettie, the groom's mother, wouldn't be at the ceremony. She would be at home getting ready for the dinner. Karen and several other women would leave, once the vows were exchanged, to act as servers for the several hundred people expected to arrive that afternoon.

At exactly nine o'clock the singing began. Bishop Zook and the two ministers escorted the bride and groom to a separate room. While they were given instructions on the duties of marriage in the Council room, the congregation sang the wedding hymns.

When the bridal couple returned, the bishop began his sermon. He spoke with simple eloquence about the marriages in the Old Testament. He spoke about Adam and Eve and proceeded to the Great Flood and the virtuousness of Noah's household. He recounted the story of Isaac and Rebekah and talked about the way God works through events to bring marriage partners together.

Bishop Zook looked at the couple and said, "God had a plan for you. You found each other because you were willing to submit to His will and to His choice."

His words brought tears to Karen's eyes. She knew the struggles Katie had endured in her life away from the Amish. It was through those circumstances that God led her and her baby daughter back to the faith and into the life of Elam Sutter.

Karen couldn't help wondering how God was using John in her life. What plan did He have for each of them? Whatever it was, it could not be marriage.

It was nearly noon before the lengthy sermon was concluded and the bishop asked Katie and Elam to step forward. They clasped hands with gentle smiles at each other. The bishop placed his hand over theirs. He pronounced a blessing upon them and asked, "Are you willing to enter together into wedlock as God in the beginning ordained and commanded?"

"Yes," they both answered in firm, solemn voices.

As he asked each of them if they were confident God had chosen the person beside them to be their husband or wife, Karen's thoughts turned again to John.

Had he made a similar vow? Had he pledged to cherish and care for a woman as a Christian husband until the Lord separated them by death? Was there someone waiting and praying to see him again?

Was there a woman whose heart skipped a beat at the sight of his smile the way hers did?

John was happy for the company of the gruff doctor when they arrived at the Sutter farm. Buggies filled every free space between the house and barn and extended down the lane. The corral overflowed with horses munching hay as they waited patiently to take families home. Everywhere, groups of women in long dresses and men in dark suits with black hats stood talking in animated conversations or were working together.

One group of adults was busy washing dishes in large red plastic tubs as a trio of young women carried out trays of dirty plates and hurried back inside with the clean ones.

The doctor had been right. There had to be over two hundred people John could speak with. He worked to temper his expectations. He'd been disappointed too many times already.

When Dr. White got out of the car the men and women standing nearby greeted him cheerfully. One, a small gnomelike man with a long white beard said, "The *goot doktor* is here. If you want free advice, step right up."

Harold clapped a hand on the old man's shoulder. "Good to see you, too, Reuben Beachy. Tell me, why did they invite an old rascal like you to this wedding?"

Reuben chuckled. "Who better to invite than a harness maker when you are getting hitched for life?"

Everyone laughed at his joke including Dr. White. Harold raised one hand and said to the group, "I will have time to hear what ails you and repeat all the gossip, but I must see the bride and groom and eat before the food is gone."

They all chuckled as Harold led the way to the house. As John entered the Sutter home, he was stunned by the transformation that had taken place inside. Wall partitions had been removed to open up all the downstairs rooms. The kitchen itself was a crush of women working.

From the front door he could see trestle tables had been lined along the kitchen walls, around three sides of the living room and even into an adjoining bedroom.

The bride and groom sat in one corner of the living room in view of everyone. Katie sat at Elam's left hand. Young women filled the tables around the couple and sat with their backs to the walls while the young men sat on the opposite side of the table facing the girls.

The tables didn't contain flowers. Rather, stalks of celery had been placed in glass jars as decoration. Candy dishes, beautiful cakes and large bowls of fruit completed the simple but festive array. John searched for Karen in the rooms but didn't see her anywhere.

Doctor White glanced at John. "Shall we start by asking the women in the kitchen if they know you?"

John's eyes were drawn to the bride and groom and the loving looks they exchanged as they visited with their friends.

He nodded toward them. "No. This is their day.

I don't want to take anything away from them. We can speak to people outside after the meal is done."

The doctor gave John a smile of approval. "All right."

A strapping Amish man with a clean-shaven face approached them. He introduced himself as Adam Troyer and asked them to follow him. He seated them at one of the bedroom tables where Amber and a tall, handsome man already faced each other.

The man with Amber rose and held out his hand. His resemblance to Harold was unmistakable. He said, "You must be John. I'm Dr. Phillip White and this old rascal is my grandfather." He clapped Harold on the shoulder.

"Who you calling old?" Harold grumbled.

"Behave," Amber warned them both with a hard look.

The men grinned at each other, but took their seats. Amber and Phillip already had their food. John and Harold didn't have to wait long. In another minute, a petite woman came in with a plate loaded with roast chicken and duck, mashed potatoes, dressing and creamed celery. She set the dish in front of Harold. John recognized her as the woman who ran the inn. She set down a second plate loaded with cookies and slices of cake.

Harold said, "Thank you, Emma. I hear the wedding was held in your home."

"*Ja,* Katie has no family here so we are her family now." She smiled at John. "Your plate is coming."

"I have it here."

John looked over his shoulder to see Karen bearing a pair of plates for him. When she set them down, his eyes grew round. "You don't expect me to eat all that, do you?"

"I do, and you will have more later. No one leaves an Amish wedding hungry."

He pushed the dessert plate toward her. "At least help me with this."

She patted her slender waist. "I ate before the wedding party arrived so that I could help serve today. I must get back to work. More guests will begin arriving shortly."

Emma said, "Why don't you take a short break? Ruby and I can handle serving for a little while. I'm sure Mr. Doe has questions about our customs. I will bring you a cup of tea."

Karen grinned. "Then I will happily cover for your break when I am done here. You may tell Adam Troyer I won't be long. I'm sure he is ready for a break, too."

Emma's flushed cheeks turned an even brighter red. She left the table without another word.

"So that's the way the wind is blowing," Harold

said with a chuckle. "I wondered why Adam was always at the inn. I thought surely there couldn't be that much work for a handyman to do around the place."

Emma returned with a cup of hot tea for Karen but didn't linger. Karen took a sip, then filched a cookie from John's plate. John leaned toward her. "Should I go wish the bride and groom happy before I eat?"

Karen shook her head. "No congratulations are given at an Amish wedding. It is taken for granted that Elam and Katie have found the partner chosen by God for them. We have no divorce so marriage is forever. Today is a happy but serious day."

In the living room, a young man with curly brown hair rose to his feet and spoke in Pennsylvania Dutch.

Dr. White said, "The first round of eating is almost over. It's time for the singing to start."

John sent Karen an inquisitive glance. "The first round of eating?"

"*Ja*, we will start the wedding supper in an hour or so. Many of the older guests will leave soon, but the young people will stay. There will be much visiting and even games out in the barn."

Around the tables, guests were bringing out their songbooks. The curly-headed young man, in a beautiful voice, started the hymn, and soon all joined in except the bride and groom. There was no accompanying music, just a moving blend of dozens of voices.

Karen asked, "Do you recognize the melody or the words?"

Was that worry he saw in her eyes? Why would she be concerned if he knew the song? He shook his head. "No, it's not familiar."

She seemed to relax. At least she gave him a half smile before joining in the hymn. Her sweet alto was pleasing to his ear. Once again he felt a deep pull of attraction toward Karen, something he couldn't put his finger on but something he wanted to hold on to. Each day he spent with her those feelings deepened.

He counted her among his very few friends. He wasn't sure she would appreciate how often he thought of her not as a friend but as a woman.

When the first song was done, a young woman stood to announce a second song. She then led the congregation. Her voice, pure and light as sunshine, flowed around the room. He listened more closely. There was something deeply familiar in her voice. Had he heard her before?

Chapter Eight

When the song ended, John touched Karen's arm and gestured toward the singer. "Who is that woman?"

"That is Sarah Wyse, why?"

"She has a beautiful voice. Could I have heard her before?"

"Where?"

"I have no idea. Does she live near you?"

"Not far. She lives just at the edge of Hope Springs. Her husband ran a harness shop. He passed away three years ago from cancer. She works in the fabric store now."

"It's strange. I just think I've heard her voice before."

"I will see if she will talk to you when the singing is done." Karen stayed for one more hymn and then returned to her duties serving the guests.

When John had eaten his fill, he excused

himself from the table and walked outside. Uncertain of how to introduce himself to the Amish and uncomfortable at being an outsider at a wedding feast, he stood alone on the porch gathering his courage. The door opened and Nettie bustled out with a large pan full of dishes.

Catching sight of him, she stopped and settled her load on one hip. "Have you had enough to eat, Mr. Doe?"

"More than enough. Thank you. Why are you working? Shouldn't you be inside enjoying your son's wedding day?"

"The parents of the bride and groom receive no special treatment on this day. It is my job to supervise the kitchen and make sure everything runs smoothly. That is my gift to my son and my new daughter. And you, Mr. Doe, you wish to speak to some of our guests, do you not?"

"I thought I did but I didn't realize I would feel so awkward about it."

She looked over to the men gathered near the barn. "Do not feel awkward. Let me get someone to take you around and introduce you."

Waving her hand toward them, she called to Eli Imhoff. "Eli, come here."

He crossed the yard with quick steps. "What do you need, Nettie?"

John couldn't help but notice the soft look that passed between them or how the color bloomed in Nettie's cheeks. She said, "John wishes to be introduced to some of our guests. I have not the time. Can you escort him for me?"

Eli nodded. "It was my intention to do so."

As Nettie carried her pan to the washing tubs, Eli followed her with his eyes. John said, "She has been very kind."

"*Ja,* she is a *goot* woman."

The door to the house opened. Several Amish couples came out followed by Harold. The elderly doctor pulled a roll of antacid tablets from his pocket. "I knew I was going to need these. The food is always so good but so rich."

He offered some to John and Eli. John declined but Eli accepted them. Dr. White said, "How is the arm, Eli?"

"Old bones heal slow."

"Tell me about it." Harold rubbed his thigh.

Eli jerked his head toward the barn. "Let us see if any one recognizes John Doe."

Harold said, "Amber and Karen are asking around inside. I thought the women would be more comfortable talking to them."

John followed the men through the maze of buggies to the barn. Inside, youngsters were engaged in games and chatting in groups. He caught sight of Jacob and several of his friends looking down from the hayloft. He was surprised to see the young men were much older than Jacob. The boy's friends were staring at John with outright curiosity and snickering.

Eli asked for everyone's attention, speaking English out of deference to John and Harold. He briefly explained John's situation and asked if anyone knew him or had seen him before. John scanned the faces of the young men and women looking for signs of recognition. The only one he knew was the freckle-faced redheaded young woman he'd met several days before.

Sally, that was her name. He smiled and nodded to her. Her eyes widened. She spoke to her friends and then hurried past him back toward the house.

He followed Eli and Harold from group to group speaking to elderly couples, young parents with children and teenagers that had paired off and were enjoying the social event. Each time he met with expressions of compassion but no concrete information.

Giving up for the moment, John excused himself from the older man and returned to the house. Something in Sally's expression stayed with him. He wanted a chance to talk to her in private but didn't know how that would be possible. He was about to open the door when Karen came out with Sarah Wyse, the singer, by her side.

* * *

Karen stopped in surprise when she saw John in front of her. "We were just coming to find you. John, this is Sarah Wyse."

The way his eyes roved over Sarah's face sent a prickle of envy through Karen. Immediately, she chided herself for allowing such emotion to taint the day. Sarah was pretty. The young men had flocked around her when she and Karen had been in school together, but none of that had gone to Sarah's head. She remained a devout member of the church in spite of all the heartache in her life.

John said, "It's nice to meet you, Mrs. Wyse. I wanted to compliment you on your beautiful singing voice."

Sarah glanced from Karen back to John. "Compliments are not needed. All gifts come from God. We do not seek honors or to stand apart from each other."

"I'm sorry," John said, "I did not mean to offend you."

"No offense was taken. Karen says you have some questions for me."

The three of them moved to the end of the porch so they weren't blocking the flow of traffic in and out of the house. John said, "I don't know how to say this, but your voice sounds familiar to me.

Is there any way I could have heard you singing before?"

"Not unless you have heard me as one of many voices praising God in song during our church services."

He heaved a tired sigh. "I was afraid you were going to say that."

"I wish I could be more help. I will inquire about you when people come to my shop. We have townspeople, Amish and tourists in."

John said, "I'll ask the sheriff to send over one of the photographs he had taken of me."

The women exchanged glances, then Karen said, "Sarah would not be able to show it. We consider photographs of people to be graven images. They are forbidden."

"I'm sorry. I didn't know." He looked embarrassed.

Karen couldn't help herself. She poked his shoulder. "Oh, John, you don't know your name, you don't know about the Amish and photographs, what do you know?"

"Karen!" Sarah looked aghast.

John looked shocked for a full second then he threw back his head and laughed. "I know if I go back in the house someone is going to try and make me eat more. I'm still stuffed to the gills."

Relieved to see him more comfortable, Karen said, "Then you had best go walk up an appetite because supper will get under way in about an hour."

Sarah said, "Mr. Doe, I can't use a photograph but if someone were to sketch your face I could use that."

Nodding Karen said, "That is a *goot* idea. Sally Yoder has a fine hand with pencils. Perhaps she could draw his picture."

John asked, "Is she the one with red hair and freckles?"

"*Ja.*" Karen looked around. "I saw her a few moments ago."

Sarah said, "I saw her go upstairs with Katie and the baby. I will ask her if she would do a sketch of you. Provided her parents do not object. If she may, I will let you know."

"I appreciate your help, Sarah. Thank you. And even if compliments are not permitted, I still say you sing like an angel."

Her smile turned sad. "You should have heard my sister sing. She is the one with the voice of an angel."

John waited until Sarah disappeared into the house then he turned his attention to Karen. "What did she mean about her sister?"

"Sarah has a twin sister. Bethany left here a month after Sarah's husband died. She wrote Sarah a letter telling her she had to go away but gave no other explanation. No one has heard from her in three years. Most think she ran away with an *Englischer*. It broke Sarah's heart."

"I see. Well, I should let you get back to work."

Karen didn't want to leave him. She wanted to stay and find some way to make him laugh again. The sound made her heart light. It made her want to laugh out loud with him.

With a start, she realized what was happening. She was getting in over her head. When had she started to care so deeply for John?

Perhaps the moment she saw him lying in the ditch. Embarrassed by the flood of feelings she couldn't control she took a step back. "*Ja*, I must go."

He raised his hand but let it drop quickly to his side. "I guess I'll see you when you get home."

"It will be very late. We will have much cleaning up to do here."

"I don't mind staying up." He smiled softly at her and left the porch to rejoin the men standing by Harold's car.

Late that evening, John sat outside on the *dawdy haus* porch with his feet propped up on the rail and his hands shoved deep in the pockets of his coat. The cold night air was a reminder that winter would come roaring in soon.

What was he doing? He was waiting to get in trouble, that's what.

The lights in the main house had been off for hours. The Imhoffs were normally early to bed and early to rise, but Karen had not yet returned from the wedding supper. Was she visiting with the women or was there a man in her life? Some tall, sturdy Amish farmer who would give her a dozen children and a lifetime of hard work?

John wanted to hope that was true, but even more he hoped it wasn't.

The clatter of horse hooves on the lane finally announced her return. John rose to his feet but hesitated. What right did he have to engage Karen's affections? The answer was abundantly clear. He had no business seeking time alone with her.

Even as his thoughts formed, his feet were moving toward the barn where she was unhitching the buggy. She saw him coming. She stood waiting, not speaking. He knew words would only sound artificial. Instead, he began unharnessing the horse, happy to be doing a simple thing for her.

Working in silence, they soon completed the task and led Molly to her stall. Karen lit a lantern so he could see to brush the mare down. He made quick work of it while Karen forked hay into the stall. When the mare was settled, they closed her stall door, put out the lantern and walked side-by-side out of the barn.

At the porch steps they paused by unspoken consent. Karen sat down, drawing her coat tighter. John sat beside her staring up into the night sky. A million twinkling stars decorated the black heavens with breathtaking beauty.

She pointed over the barn. "Look, there is a falling star. You should make a wish."

Hunching his shoulders, he shook his head. "I don't believe in wishing."

"Why not?"

He gazed at her intently. "What good does it do to want a thing you cannot have?"

She drew the edges of her coat closer together. "When we say we wish the rain would stop, or we wish the sun would shine, or we wish you could remember, are these wishes not simply little prayers?"

"I guess they are."

"Don't you believe in the power of prayer?"

"Anna told me once that you remind her to pray. Are you trying to remind me now?"

"It is something we all need to do."

He leaned back and braced his elbows on the step behind him. "I don't remember how to pray. If I ever knew."

"But you did. The day I found you, you began the Twenty-third Psalm. I've prayed it with you."

"You did? I wish I could remember that." He drank in the beauty of her face in the starlight, gathering in every detail to save in his memory. This night was one he never wanted to forget.

He leaned toward her. Uncertainty clouded her eyes and she looked away.

He drew a deep breath and leaned his head back. "I don't remember the stars looking this beautiful."

"Perhaps you lived in a city where the stars could not be seen."

"Maybe." John shook his head. "I don't know, they just don't seem right."

She looked up. "What could be wrong with the wondrous night sky God has given us? I see nothing wrong with the stars. What do you mean?"

"I don't know. I look up and I think something is missing."

"The moon is not yet up. Perhaps that is what's missing."

He watched her intently. "Maybe the stars look wrong because they pale in comparison to your eyes."

"Please don't." She dropped her gaze to stare at the ground.

"I'm sorry." He'd meant every word, but he was sorry to cause her any distress.

"You're forgiven."

"I'm not sure I want to be forgiven for telling

you what a beautiful person you are. I don't mean just beautiful on the outside, although you are. I mean you're beautiful on the inside."

She raised her gaze to his. "You told me that once before. That I was beautiful. The day I found you. Before the ambulance came."

"Did you believe me then?"

"I did," she answered quietly.

"And do you believe me now?" He held his breath waiting for her answer.

"This is foolishness." She surged to her feet and started to go inside but he caught her arm.

"Please don't go. We'll talk about something else. We'll pretend we're two old friends having a pleasant visit. You are my only friend, you know."

She studied his face. "I know I am now, but you have other friends who are looking for you. You are not a man who cuts himself off from others. They will find you."

"And what if they don't? What if no one is looking for me? What if I'll always be alone?" He couldn't stop the quiver in his voice. The fear and the loneliness bottled up inside rose to choke him.

She reached out to cup his face. "Do not give up hope."

Closing his eyes he covered her hands with his own and pressed them against his face, feeling the warmth and the strength and the compassion in her touch. Unbidden, a tear slipped from the corner of his eye.

Suddenly her arms were around him and she was holding him tight. "Be not afraid, John Doe, for God is with you. You are never alone."

Wrapping his arms around her, he leaned into her strength. She comforted him as if he were a child, murmuring soft sounds of reassurance. He tried to choke back his tears, but it was no use.

Chapter Nine

Karen held John tightly, her heart aching for him. All she had wanted from the moment she first saw him was to help him. She couldn't imagine the suffering he had endured and was still enduring. He was in so much pain, but she didn't know how to help.

He clung to her like a drowning man. His shoulders shook with muffled sobs. Offering him what comfort she could, she stroked his hair and whispered, "It will be okay."

But would it be? She had faith in God's plan for his life, but she knew that didn't mean his life would be easy. Her own family was proof of that, but God had not abandoned them. He gave them strength and hope. Without her faith, it would have been impossible for her to go on.

John regained his composure before she was

ready to let him go. Stepping away from her, he wiped his eyes on his sleeves. "I'm sorry."

"Don't be, John. You have the right to grieve."

"I didn't mean to fall apart like that."

"Are you sure you're okay?" She was shocked at how much she wanted to be needed by him. Shocked by how much she wanted to hold him and to be held by him.

He shoved his hands in his pockets and avoided making eye contact. "The doctors warned me that I might have a meltdown. Stress, you know. I guess I should have warned you, but I didn't expect to start blubbering like a baby."

Stepping back, he said, "Don't let me keep you up any later, Karen. You've had a long day. I'll be fine."

"Many times I have found my burdens too heavy to bear. Tears help sometimes and so do prayers. Pray for strength, John."

"I'll try. Thanks. For everything." He turned away and entered the grandfather house as if he couldn't wait to get away.

Karen climbed the steps slowly and entered her kitchen. Inside, she closed the door and leaned against it, crossing her arms tightly.

Her collar was damp from John's tears. She could still smell the faint scent of the soap he used, still feel his lingering warmth on her skin.

Never in her life had she been drawn to a man the way she was drawn to John.

In a stunning moment of clarity she realized her feelings had progressed far beyond wanting to help him. The emotions filling her heart and mind were those a woman saved for the man she was to marry.

Tears pricked at the back of her eyes. She blinked hard to hold them at bay.

It was wrong. Wrong to feel so much for someone not of her faith. How did it happen? How could she have been blind to the changes in her own heart?

She knew right from wrong. She recognized her need to be with John, to be held in his arms, to touch his face, those things were wrong.

In her mind she knew it—but her heart would not agree.

Any relationship between them was doomed. She knew that, but did John? Had she inadvertently set him up for more disappointment? She couldn't bear the thought of hurting him more than he was already hurting.

"What am I going to do?" she whispered in the darkness.

To step outside the *Ordnung,* the rules of her faith, was to invite heartache for her and her entire family. She had others to think of. Her father had been through so much pain already. She could not add to his overburdened shoulders the shame of having a daughter shunned.

Straightening, she moved across the room and up the stairs, listening to the familiar creak of each tread, hoping not to wake anyone. After reaching her room, she got ready for bed and lay beneath the heavy quilt her mother had stitched. Somehow, she had to find a way to harden her heart against the temptation she faced. John would leave tomorrow afternoon when Emma had room for him at the inn. Until he was gone, Karen would guard her heart closely. No one must know how she felt.

Closing her eyes, she prayed for strength. It was a long time before she fell asleep.

John sat at the desk in his room listening to the hushed stillness of the night. Like a hamster in a wheel, his brain ran around and around the problems he faced, without generating any answers.

His breakdown tonight scared him more than he wanted to admit. Was the stress unhinging his mind? Could he face the fact that he might never remember his life from before?

It had been nearly three weeks since Karen found him. He had visited Amish and English farms all along Pleasant View Road. He'd spoken to dozens of families, and yet he was no closer to the answers he needed. No one knew who he was. How could he not be missed? Why wasn't someone looking for him?

A chilling thought brought his overworked brain to a screeching halt. Maybe no one cared enough about him to wonder where he was.

What kind of man had he been? What kind of man wasn't missed by anyone?

Panic rushed through him until he recalled Karen's voice telling him he should pray for strength. He wanted to have faith in God's goodness, but that was easier said than done.

He bowed his head, resting it on his folded hands, and spoke the words in his heart. "God, I'm floundering here. I've got no idea what You want from me. Karen says I need Your help and I believe her. She is the one good thing You've done for me.

"I can't face this alone. You know I want answers. If I get them or not, well, that's up to You. Just give me the strength to accept whatever comes and keep me from going insane."

Raising his head, he drew a deep cleansing breath. Nothing had changed except for one small fact. Whatever happened, he didn't have to face it alone.

The chill in the air soon drove him under the covers. Lying in bed, he knew he needed a new plan. The money he had wouldn't last much longer. He could afford another week, maybe two at the inn in Hope Springs when he left here, but then what?

One more unanswerable question. He wanted to scream with frustration. Rolling to his side, he resolved to stop worrying about the future and have faith.

He slept fitfully the rest of the night. It was still dark outside when he gave up. Dressing in the chilly room he chided himself for not banking the fire the previous night. The stove was stone cold when he checked it and the wood box was empty.

Pausing on the front porch, he glanced at the main house. All the windows were still dark, even the ones upstairs. He wasn't sure which one was Karen's bedroom but he knew she would be up soon.

How would she treat him after seeing him break down last night? Would she think less of him? Did she see him as weak, now? Her opinion mattered. Maybe more than it should.

After carrying in an armload of wood, John set to work rebuilding the fire. When he had a small blaze going, he closed the firebox door and straightened, noticing his ribs didn't protest the movement. Physically, he was healing.

Mentally? Not so much. He needed something to do. Something to keep him busy besides endlessly turning over every rock in his mind looking for his memory.

A sudden idea occurred to him. Karen's father needed help with the chores. Horses were something John seemed to know about. He glanced out the window toward the barn. He was up, he might as well lend Eli a hand.

He was in the barn thirty minutes later when Jacob and Noah came in yawning and with lagging steps.

"Morning," John called cheerfully. He finished shoveling out the last stall, then laid his pitchfork and shovel on top of the heaping wheelbarrow.

"What do you think you're doing?" Jacob demanded.

"Mucking out the stalls." John started toward the rear of the barn.

Noah grinned and fell into step beside John. "Yippee. Now I don't have to do it."

Jacob chided Noah in Pennsylvania Dutch. John understood the tone if not the actual words.

Noah's grin turned to a scowl. "I'm going to help Jacob with the milking."

Looking over Noah's head, John said, "I have one more stall to do. If you want to show me how to milk a cow I could help with that, too."

"We do not need your help, English." Jacob took his younger brother by the sleeve and pulled him toward the dairy cows patiently waiting by their stanchions.

After dumping his wheelbarrow load, John returned to the last stall. Slipping a halter on One-Way's head, John led him out to the small paddock and turned him loose. Snorting and prancing, One-Way showed his appreciation of the open space by bucking his way around the enclosure.

Smiling at the animal's high spirits, John said, "Work off a little of that ginger and maybe we'll try some training later."

One-Way trotted to the fence. Stretching his neck over the top boards, he playfully nipped at John's sleeve, then took off like a rocket.

"I don't care what you think of the plan," John shouted after him. "There's a harness in your future. You'd better get used to the idea."

Chuckling to himself, John finished cleaning One-Way's stall. After making sure all of the horses had hay, grain and freshwater, he brought the young Standardbred back in. Locking the stall door, John leaned on it admiring the horse.

Behind him, he heard Anna say, "There you are, John Doe. Have you forgotten where the house is?"

Stifling his amusement, John crouched in front of her. "I'm so glad you found me. I thought I was going to have to stay out here with the horses all day. Which way do I go?"

Anna shook her head as she grasped his hand. "Come, I will show you. Breakfast is ready."

"Thank you." Rising, he let the child lead the way, but stopped when he saw Eli watching them.

Anna said, "I found him, Papa. He forgot where the house was."

Eli's lips twitched. "Thank you, Anna. Run along and tell Karen we are coming."

"Hurry up 'cause I'm hungry." She headed toward the house at a run.

Eli moved to the nearest stall where a pretty brown mare with a white star greeted him. "Noah tells me you did his chores."

"I hope you don't mind. I felt the need to work. I've loafed long enough."

"Work is *goot* for a man's body and soul."

"It felt good. It felt right."

Eli turned away from his inspection of John's work and began walking toward the house. "What are your plans now?"

John fell into step beside him. "I've talked to just about everyone in the community and I've come up empty. I guess I need to find work and a place to live now. I'm not giving up hope. I'm just being practical."

Eli combed his fingers through his beard. "A job will not be easy to come by this time of year. What kind of work were you thinking of doing?"

"All I seem to know is horses."

"I see. How would you break a green horse to harness?"

John answered without thinking. "You don't break a horse. You train it."

Eli eyed John critically. "That is true. How would you go about training that bay mare with the white star?"

"The first thing I'd do is get her used to having a blanket thrown over her. Then I'd work up to a partial and finally a full harness," he replied almost by rote. Each step closer to the house and to Karen increased John's dread. His palms grew sweaty.

Eli said, "That is what I would do, too."

They reached the front porch and climbed the steps. John pulled open the door. Eli went in while John hesitated on the doorstep.

What would he say to Karen? How would she treat him? He rubbed his damp palms on the sides of his jeans.

Suddenly, she was standing in front of him. She held a pan of cinnamon bread with the corners of her apron. "Close the door, John Doe. You're letting the cold air in," she scolded. "And don't forget to wipe your feet."

Noah and Anna, already seated at the table, snickered into their hands.

Whirling around, she scowled at them and placed the pan on the kitchen table before moving back to the stove.

John relaxed a little. Okay, good. Apparently she wasn't going to walk on eggshells around him. He wiped his feet, washed his hands at the sink and took his place at the table. A moment later she took her place opposite him. Everyone bowed their heads for silent prayer.

When they were finished, Karen looked at John and said, "Pass the butter, please."

No lingering glance, no pitying look, just pass the butter, as if nothing had happened. He appreciated her effort to put him at ease.

Everyone started eating. As usual, there was very little conversation at the table. Mealtime was for eating. John had learned that talk revolved mainly around what chores needed to be done and plans for the upcoming events such as the horse auction.

When the meal was finished, Anna helped Karen clear the table. Eli retreated to the sitting room to read his paper while Jacob and Noah finished getting ready for school. John remained at the table nursing his cup of coffee.

Anna gathered the tableware slowly, casting several speculative glances at John. Finally he asked, "What is it, Anna?"

"If I invite you to our school Christmas program, will you be able to remember that?"

He rubbed his hand over his chin. "I think if I write it down I'll be able to remember. When is it?"

"It's on December twenty-fourth."

"Christmas Eve, I'm sure I won't forget that. Have you been a good girl this year? Do you think Santa Claus will bring you presents?"

Anna laid a comforting hand on John's arm. "There is no Santa Claus. Did you forget that, too?"

Karen rinsed a plate and set it in the drain board. "We do not believe in such things, John. For us, Christmas is a time to remember the birth of Christ."

"You don't exchange gifts?" he asked.

"Little things only on the day after Christmas," Karen said. "It is a time to visit with family and friends."

"Last year I got new mittens," Anna added with a bright smile.

He wished he could remember a Christmas past. Would it ever end, these constant reminders that he was an incomplete man?

* * *

Karen saw the change come over John's face. Before she could think of something to say he shot to his feet and said, "Have a good day at school, Anna. I won't forget about your Christmas program."

He lifted his coat from the hook by the door and was gone a second later. Karen wanted to run after him but she didn't. He would have to come to grips with his missing memories in his own fashion.

Smiling at Anna, Karen said, "Go get ready for school."

Before long she had all the children out the door. That first minute of blessed silence afterward was always the best part of her day. She finished wiping down the counters and the table and had just started sweeping the floor when her father came in from the sitting room.

"Where is John?" Eli asked.

She didn't look up from her sweeping. "I don't know. He left about five minutes before the children."

"I'm thinking of letting him stay on a little longer."

Karen looked up in surprise. "You are?"

"*Ja.*" Eli stared at her.

She started sweeping again. "If he stays it will

make more work for me, but we could use the extra money."

"He seems to know a lot about horses." Eli slipped into his coat and pulled it over his sling.

Moving a chair, she swept under the table. She couldn't believe her father was considering this. "Perhaps he could be some help to you. Until your arm heals."

"Maybe."

Karen swept her pile of dirt into the dustpan without looking up. "He may not want to stay."

"Why do you think that?"

She straightened to meet her father's gaze. "Plain living is hard for the English. He may want to live where he can have television, a phone or a computer."

"I've not heard him complain about living plain, have you?"

"*Nee,* but he often goes into Hope Springs to use the computer at the library."

"Well, if he wishes it, he may stay. I will tell him." Eli opened the door and went out.

Karen backed up until she located a chair, then she sat down abruptly.

Would John stay?

Did she want him to stay?

The simple, frightening answer was yes, she did. With sudden clarity she saw exactly what she must do.

* * *

John stuffed the last of his meager possessions into his duffel bag. He started to close the top when he heard Eli call his name. He answered, "I'm in the bedroom."

Eli appeared in the doorway. "John Doe, I have a proposition for you."

"What kind of proposition?"

"I've been thinking. If you want, you could stay here until you find a job."

"Stay here?" John wasn't sure he'd heard correctly.

Eli winced and adjusted his sling. "I could use help getting the horses ready to sell. A horse that is trained to harness will bring more money than one that is not."

John buckled his bag. "Jacob can help you with that."

"Jacob must go to school, and he is already doing many more of the chores that I cannot do."

"What if I can't actually train a horse? I mean, I only feel like I know how."

"We can work together. My arm is broken but my voice works. I will tell you what to do and you do it?"

John was so very tempted to say yes. This family had opened their home to him. He was comfortable here. Karen was here.

That was why he should go.

"Think it over," Eli suggested before John could say anything.

Eli turned to leave but John stopped him with a question. "Have you told Karen about this?"

Chapter Ten

Eli gave John a sharp look. "*Ja*, I told Karen I would offer to let you stay on."

"And she was okay with it?"

"She offered no objection. Why?"

Was that because she felt sorry for him or because she liked having him around? He wished he could ask her. "I don't want to make more work for your daughter."

Eli cracked a wide smile. "She did say you would make extra work, but she also said we can use the money."

John ran a hand through his hair. "Depend on Karen to tell the truth."

"She speaks her mind. It is a thing she learned from her mother."

John quickly made up his own mind. He walked toward Eli and held out his hand. "I will stay on one condition. If I'm going to be working for you I expect to pay less for rent."

Eli's smile widened. "We had best agree on this before Karen gets wind of it."

"Before I get wind of what?" Her voice came from down the hall.

John braced himself to face her and pretend he wasn't thrilled to be spending more time near her. He had nowhere to go. He apparently had no one who cared about him. So why shouldn't he find some measure of happiness in the new life he'd been given?

"Looks like you aren't getting rid of me just yet," he called out.

She appeared in the doorway beside her father, her face serene and composed. "Then strip the sheets from the bed while I get clean ones and hurry up. I don't have all day."

Spinning on her heels, she took off down the hall and John heard the front door slam. He looked at Eli. "Are you sure she doesn't object to my staying?"

"I would bundle up the sheets and have them ready for her if I were you." Chuckling, Eli hooked his thumb under his suspender.

Feeling bemused, John stripped the bed. When Karen returned with the clean sheets neatly folded in a laundry basket John held the wadded ones under his arm.

She bustled in, put the basket on the bed and pulled the sheets out of it. "Put the dirty ones in here." She indicated the basket with a nod.

Eli said, "Since you are going to stay, John Doe, I will turn on the refrigerator for you. It can be tricky to get started."

As Eli headed for the kitchen, John stuffed his armload of linens in the basket then lifted it off the mattress so Karen could get to work. With a few flicks of her wrists, she spread the crisp white linen over the mattress and smoothed away the wrinkles.

As she was tucking in the far side, John set the laundry basket on the desk, turned the desk chair around and straddled it. Crossing his arms over the ladder-back, he rested his chin on his forearms. "Was this your idea? Not that I'm complaining, I'm just curious."

She shook out the second sheet and let it settle over the bed. "It was not my idea."

Disappointment pricked him but he refused to show it. "You're okay with it, right?"

"Of course." She wouldn't meet his gaze. Instead, she kept her eyes on the task she was performing.

"It won't be forever. Once I find a job I'll be able to get a place of my own." He knew he was being overly optimistic but he didn't want her caring out of pity.

Stuffing the pillow into the case, she shook it down. "What kind of work will you do?"

"Whatever it takes. I don't have much choice. I have to make my own way now."

She paused, clutching the pillow tight to her chest. "I wish you well, John Doe."

Was that a quiver he heard in her voice? He said, "Someday I will repay all that you have done for me."

Turning to face him, she shook her head. "*Nee*, you owe me nothing. I will do everything I can to help you find a job."

Was she hinting that she wanted him to move on? "Any suggestions where I should start?"

"The newspaper."

"Right. I can see the ad now. Wanted: Man with amnesia for high-paying job."

Throwing the pillow on the bed, Karen propped her hands on her hips and scowled at him. "With that attitude you will end up begging on street corners."

Taken aback, he said, "I was joking."

She kept her voice low as she glanced toward the door to make sure Eli wasn't outside. "Finding a livelihood is no joking matter. You must be serious, you must work harder and smarter than anyone else and prove you can do the job."

John held up both hands in a gesture of surrender. "Okay, I will."

"If you go around feeling sorry for yourself then your life will be filled with pity and not with the blessings God has bestowed upon you."

Anger welled up inside him. "Excuse me for not feeling blessed at the moment."

She took a step toward him. "Well, you should feel blessed. You are alive. You are strong. You have a roof over your head and food to eat. If you whine about the things you do not have then you are ungrateful for all you have."

Why was she trying to rile him? He said, "I have all these things because of the charity of others. I did not earn it."

She folded her arms and raised her eyebrow. "And that is not a blessing?"

Rising from the chair, he turned to the window. Bracing his arms on the sill he stared outside. "I don't want to be grateful to others. I need to be in charge of my own life."

She moved to stand close behind him. "Then pride is your sin, John Doe. The Amish live humble lives. We accept that we are nothing without God."

John's anger drained away. He understood better than most what being *nothing* felt like. Looking over his shoulder at Karen, he asked, "Do you think that's why God is doing this to me? To humble me? What kind of person was I to deserve this?"

Karen bit her lip, drawing his attention to her mouth. He wanted to kiss her, wanted to hold her and feel her arms around him. As much as her compassion meant to him that wasn't what he longed for. He wanted more.

He wanted her to care about him as a man, not as an emotional cripple in need of charity.

She looked down and fixed her gaze on her clenched hands. "We cannot know God's plan for us. It is beyond human understanding. We can only accept what trials come to us secure in the knowledge that God is with us always. He sent His only son to die for our sins. He does not abandon us. We lean on His mercy and grace so that we may not stumble on the righteous path He sets before us."

"I wish I had your faith, Karen. I wish I believed in mercy and grace."

She did look at him then. "You have only to open your heart to God, John. All the rest will follow."

The soft expression in her eyes gave him hope. She did care for him, he was sure of it.

"How can I doubt God's goodness when He brought me to you." He reached for her as he stepped closer.

She took a quick step away. "John, we can't—I can't. How do I say this? There must be no closeness between us."

Her retreat cut him like a blade. Lowering his hand, he closed his eyes and pressed his lips into a thin, painful line. Finally, he drew a deep breath and nodded. "I understand. I'm sorry if I offended you with unwelcome attention."

"There is nothing to forgive. I am your friend."

How could such simple words sound so lame?

What had he expected? She was a devout Amish woman. She would never consider stepping outside the boundaries of her faith with someone like him. She offered her friendship. He would be content with that. It was more than he deserved.

At the sound of Eli's footsteps coming down the hall, John quickly composed himself. He fashioned a reassuring smile for her. "I couldn't find a better friend if I searched the world over," he said, meaning every word.

Karen blinked hard to hold back her tears. They would have to wait until later, when she was alone and no one could hear her sobs. They would be her punishment for wounding John. In spite of his words, she knew she had wounded him.

At every turn she had sought to guard him from harm, to ease his way, to be the one person he could turn to. Her foolish need to be his rescuer had led to this affection for her. How could it be otherwise? Perhaps in her heart she even wanted such affection, but it wasn't right for either of them.

She had to let John find his own path and his own strength. The only way to do that was to push him out into the world.

"Your refrigerator is working now," Eli announced from the doorway.

John slipped the chair in place under the desk. The sudden silence seemed to radiate guilt. Karen quickly picked up the laundry basket and walked out the door without looking back. She had never felt so ashamed of her own weakness.

That night she prayed for strength and the courage to harden her heart against the attraction she felt for John. Confused and frightened, she knew only God's help could save her from her own foolishness.

If John recovered his memory she could let him go knowing he had people and a home waiting for him. But while he was still lost and alone, she couldn't turn her back on him. She couldn't.

On Sunday morning she accompanied her family to church services and prayed earnestly for strength and guidance. The saving grace of the weekend was having the children underfoot to minimize the risk of finding herself alone with John.

On Sunday afternoon, Sarah Wyse arrived with Sally Yoder to sketch a picture of John. Sally seemed oddly ill at ease. As John posed for his portrait, he tried to engage her in conversation, but he received only the briefest of replies in return.

When Sally was done, John thanked her, then left the room saying he had work to do. Sally began to put away her materials.

Karen picked up the sketch. "This is *goot* work, Sally. God has given you a wondrous talent. I know John is grateful for your help."

"I must do all I can to aid him." When Sally looked up Karen was surprised to see her eyes glistening with unshed tears.

"Sally, do you know who John is?"

Glancing from Sarah to Karen, Sally shook her head. "I don't. I wish I did, but I don't." Before Karen could question her further, Sally grabbed her sketchbook and hurried outside.

Karen and Sarah exchanged puzzled looks. Sarah said, "She is young and she has a tender heart. This outsider's injury and burdens touch us all."

Nodding, Karen let the subject drop unwilling to discuss her own feelings for John.

Sarah gathered her cloak and gloves. "I promise to have copies of this made and post them around town. Perhaps it will bring someone forward, but I hope John isn't holding his breath."

Karen knew she would be holding hers. She no longer prayed that someone would recognize him.

These days, she prayed only to keep her heart and her faith intact.

During the next week the first heavy snowfall of winter arrived, coating the fields and farms in a flawless, glittering white blanket. Winter was tightening its grip on the Ohio countryside as Christmas loomed only weeks away.

In spite of her determination to stifle her affection for John, her eyes were drawn constantly to wherever he was. When she was in the kitchen, she kept watch on the corrals beside the barn where John, under the direction of her father, began training the little bay mare named Jenny and One-Way, her father's great hope for their financial recovery.

To Karen's surprise, her father appeared to enjoy working with John. She often heard them deep in conversations about horse care and training methods and occasionally saw them laughing together. If John had been Amish she would have been thrilled to see the relationship growing between the two. But he wasn't Amish and no matter how much Eli liked him, he would never accept him as a suitor for Karen.

Anna and Noah had been delighted when they learned John would be staying. Jacob kept his opinion to himself, but it was easy for Karen to see he was upset. Especially after he learned Eli was letting John train the horses. Karen would have been happier if Jacob had expressed his unhappiness in words. Instead, he became withdrawn and secretive.

On Monday morning, Karen came down early to start breakfast and caught Jacob sneaking into the house just before dawn. Staring at his disheveled clothes, she asked, "Jacob, what have you been doing?"

"Nothing." He avoided looking at her and hurried up to his room.

Amish teenagers, especially boys, were expected to rebel against the strict rules they were raised with. She held her tongue, but decided to keep a closer watch on her brother. He was growing up too fast for her liking.

As the days passed, Karen began to relax. There had been no repeat of her closeness with John. Perhaps his initial attraction to her had worn off. She could only hope so. In spite of her prayers her feelings had only grown stronger.

John went out daily to visit other farms and to look for work. She knew he stopped frequently in Hope Springs to check the missing-persons website he'd told her about. In a way, it was hard to watch him go out into the world without her help, but she knew it was what he needed to do.

In the evenings, the family gathered in the sitting room after supper. Tonight, as had become the norm, Noah and John were engaged in a board game. Eli and Jacob were reading while Anna played with her doll on the windowsill.

Karen worked on her seemingly endless pile of mending as she covertly watched John. He seemed so at home among them. He was good with the little ones, especially Noah. John would make a fine father someday.

At that thought, she turned her mind elsewhere. Down that path lay only heartache. Glancing at Anna, Karen frowned. The child had both hands pressed against the frosty windowpane. As Karen watched, Anna glanced over her shoulder, then crept up behind Noah and put her hands on the back of his neck.

"Ach!" He jerked away, and she broke into loud giggles.

"*'Sis kald heit.*" Anna extended her hands toward John.

He pulled away in mock terror. "What does that mean?"

Noah shivered as he rubbed the back of his neck. "She said, 'It is cold today,' but what she means is she's a sneaky jerk."

"Noah," Eli chided. "Do not call your sister names. Anna, do not trouble your brother."

The siblings made sour faces at each other when Eli returned to his reading.

"What is this in Pennsylvania Dutch?" John patted his head.

"Your *kobb*," Noah replied.

"And this?" John pulled up a lock of hair.

"*Hoah*," Anna answered quickly.

John repeated the word then held up his hand. "What do you call this?"

"Hand," Noah said before Anna could.

John shook his head at the boy. "No, come on. What's the Amish word for hand?"

Noah and Anna fell into a fit of giggles. Even Eli gave a little chuckle. John glanced at Karen, a questioning look on his face. She stifled her mirth at his confusion. "The Amish word for hand *is* hand, John."

He began laughing, too. "At least I don't have to learn all new words to learn Amish. That should make it easier. Give me another that's the same."

"English." Jacob's tone made the word sound like an insult as he rose and walked out of the room.

Anna shook her head. "It's *Englisch*. That one's close but it's not the same. Fox, that's the same."

Eli laid down his book. "Bushel."

"Blind," Karen said, racking her brain for more identical words.

"Land," Anna supplied one more.

"What I need is a teacher." John was looking at Karen when he said it. She caught a glimpse of longing in his eyes, but he looked away so quickly she knew he was trying to hide it from her.

Sadness crept into her chest. They were both struggling to mask their true feelings. How long could they keep up this charade?

Anna said, "I will be your *teetshah*. You can use my schoolbooks."

John smiled at Anna, but Karen saw the effort it took. Her heart broke for him all over again.

On a Sunday morning nearly a month after his arrival at the farm John watched the Imhoff family leave for church from the window of the grandfather house kitchen. For a moment he was tempted to go with them, but he wasn't sure an English person would be welcome.

He had learned from Anna, his new and devoted teacher of all things Amish, that the Amish had no church buildings. They held their services in the homes of members rotating the services from house to house every other week.

He'd also learned the Imhoffs wouldn't be back until early afternoon as a meal always followed the services. As far as he was concerned, that left him with far too much time on his hands. He didn't like being alone.

Had he always been that way? Or was it a new condition brought on by his trauma?

Picking up his Bible, he read for an hour,

absorbing the words and trying to see how they applied to his own life. For a while his restless spirit was calmed, but eventually he closed the book and started looking for something else to do.

His options were limited. On Sunday the library in Hope Springs would be closed. He'd already made several trips into town to check the NamUs website, but he hadn't found anyone looking for a man of his description. The stories in the news and on the website about loved ones who'd vanished without a trace were as depressing as not finding information about himself. How could so many people disappear? How could he be one of them?

Slipping into his coat, he bundled up against the cold and headed out to the barn. He'd been unable to find work yet and so had spent more time training the horses than they really needed but it was something he enjoyed.

When he opened the door, a gray tomcat, one of the dozen or so that kept the rodent population under control, sat in the center aisle licking his paw. Music started playing. John heard the tinkling sounds of a waltz as if it were coming from a music box.

A sharp pain stabbed his temple. He squeezed his eyes shut. Suddenly, he was in a sunlit room with a large window. A white cat lay curled on a window-seat cushion in a patch of sunlight. As John watched, the animal stood, stretched with lazy feline grace, then jumped to the floor. Once there, it padded over to sit beside the front door. John heard a key in the lock. He sucked in a breath knowing the door was about to open. Blind dread filled his mind.

A loud whinny erased the scene.

John found himself staring at the empty center aisle of the Imhoff barn. The music was gone. He stumbled forward until he reached One-Way's stall. There, he leaned against the door drawing in harsh gulps of air to fill his starving lungs.

"Are you okay?" The tentative question came from overhead. John looked up to see Jacob staring at him from the hayloft. He heard the sound of footsteps moving away, but he couldn't see anyone else.

"Not really." Closing his eyes, John willed his racing heart to slow. The searing pain in his head died away bit by bit.

"What's the matter with you?"

John's first thought was to say nothing, but he stopped himself. Why lie to the boy? He began massaging his temples with his fingertips. "Sometimes I get memory flashes. When I do it hurts."

Jacob looked skeptical. "Did you remember who you are?"

"I never remember anything that will help me. I know this is weird, but did you hear music just now?"

Jacob sat on the edge of the opening and let his feet dangle, sending a shower of straw onto John's head. "What did you remember?"

Brushing the straw from his hair, John said, "I remembered a white cat sitting in the window. I remember the sound of a music box. Nothing that helps me figure out who I am. I'm beginning to wonder if I'll ever know."

Hearing a noise, John looked up to see Jacob lower himself from the hayloft floor. He hung for a second by his hands then dropped lightly down beside John. Jacob adjusted his black hat and said, "You should go back to the English world where you belong."

As Jacob turned and sauntered toward the door, John caught a whiff of cigarette smoke. "Who else was up there with you?"

Jacob didn't reply. It seemed he wasn't about to rat on his friends.

John yelled after him, "Why aren't you at church?"

"Why aren't you?" came Jacob's reply. He walked out of the barn without looking back.

John muttered to himself, "Because I don't know if I belong in church. I don't know where God wants me."

Opening One-Way's stall, John snapped a lead to his halter and went to lead the young horse outside to the exercise corral. As he passed by Molly's stall, he glanced in. The mare stood in the corner, her head drooping and flecks of foam speckling her chest.

Tying up One-Way, John stepped into the stall with Molly. She still bore the sweaty marks of her harness. It was odd because the family had used a different horse to pull the buggy that morning.

John glanced in the direction Jacob had gone. The boy shouldn't have left Molly in this condition. Annoyed with the thoughtless teenager, John quickly curried the mare and walked her until she was cooled down completely.

When he was finished, he took One-Way out to the exercise pen and turned the horse loose. Folding his arms on the top rail, John watched the young horse pacing proudly around the ring.

It had been more than a month since John's injury. Five full weeks without answers. He'd spent day after day searching his mind for things that were not there. Karen believed God had brought him here for a purpose. What purpose? The question circled his mind the way the horse circled the paddock.

John shoved his hands in the pockets of his coat. In spite of his occasional flashbacks, his hopes of recovery faded with each passing day. He had to face the facts. What if he never recovered his memory, never found his past?

What if God had a reason for making him forget that past? What if his former life had been so terrible that he couldn't face it? Perhaps his amnesia was a blessing and not a curse.

Could he accept that? Right now, right this minute, could he decide to stop searching?

Hadn't he already found everything he needed here? This was a place where he could make a new life. As wild as it once seemed, he could have an Amish life.

Was this what God had in mind for him? Was that why He'd brought Karen into John's life? To show him a devout, simple way to live with God at the center of everything?

John chewed the corner of his bottom lip. He was happy here. He felt he belonged here. Should he be asking for more than that?

In the beginning he'd prayed for any crumb of information about himself. Now, he knew giving up his past was the only way he could fashion a life Karen could find acceptable. Was he willing to do that?

Chapter Eleven

Seated among the women on one of the narrow wooden benches at the preaching service, Karen glanced across the aisle, looking for her brother. Her father and Noah were seated among the men but she couldn't see Jacob. Once again her heart grew troubled as her worry about him intensified. He had come ahead bringing the bench wagon to the Beachy farm, but Karen had not seen him since they arrived.

At the front of the room the bishop began speaking. Forced to give up her search she turned her attention to the preacher. Bishop Zook, in a solemn voice, announced the banns of Adam Troyer and Emma Wadler. The wedding was to take place the Thursday before Christmas.

There were quite a few soft murmurs of surprise from the congregation. Emma had long been considered an old maid in their community. At thirty-three she was still single but God had seen fit to bring the right man into her life. Karen had suspected as much but hadn't known for sure. Amish couples frequently dated and planned their engagements in secret.

Although Karen was happy for her cousin, she couldn't help the twinge of envy that marred her joy. Chiding herself for the selfish thought, Karen decided she should take it as a sign that someday God could bring the right man into her life when the children were grown and able to manage without her.

The Sunday service lasted nearly three hours. Afterward, as the men set up tables and the women began unpacking the food for the meal, Karen and Anna followed the crowd of young people into the barn. They would have to wait their turn to eat. The elders would be served first.

Anna took off to play with several of her school friends. Looking around, Karen spied Emma and Adam being congratulated. Beyond the pair she caught sight of Jacob at last. She breathed a sigh of relief until she saw he was with a group of older boys.

They were all fast boys, known to be trouble-makers and a worry to their parents. Karen wasn't happy to see Jacob so comfortable among them. The ringleader was Henry Zook, the bishop's youngest son, a young man who should know better.

Karen joined the group around Emma and Adam and spent a pleasant half hour listening to Adam's family tease him about giving up his bachelor ways.

Later, on their way home in the early afternoon Karen noticed her father had become unusually quiet. He'd had his cast removed the day before, but he still wore his arm in a sling. Checking on her siblings, Karen saw Anna and Noah were dozing in the backseat. Jacob followed behind them with the bench wagon.

Karen said, "Is something wrong, Papa? Is your arm hurting?"

"What?" He sat up straight. Karen could've sworn he looked guilty about something.

"I asked if your arm was bothering you?"

"*Nee,* it is fine. Did you know that Emma and Adam Troyer planned to marry?"

Karen smiled. "I knew something was up between them. I'm sure they will be happy. They have both waited a long time to find the right person."

"A man is blessed indeed to find a woman who will make his house a home. I pray God grants them many children." He fell silent again. Karen couldn't shake the feeling that something was troubling him.

"You had best tell me now, Papa. You know I will find out." Had he learned something about John? Was he trying to tell her that John would be leaving?

His eyes grew round as saucers. "What do you mean?"

"You have something on your mind. I see the signs. Whatever it is, do not be afraid to tell me."

He nodded, then said slowly, "*Ja,* you will find out."

"And you are afraid I'll be upset? I won't, Papa."

"Very well. I have asked Nettie Sutter to marry me and she has accepted my offer."

Karen stared at him in blank astonishment. Whatever she had been expecting, it was not this. "You're getting married?"

Exactly where did that leave her?

The words seemed to rush out of him. "I have wanted to ask her for many months. Then I broke my arm and lost the feeling in my hand. I knew I couldn't ask her to marry a man unable to support her or his own children. But God has seen fit to heal me and I thank Him for that. Today, when I heard the bishop publish the banns for Emma I felt it was the right time to approach Nettie. She said yes. She will make a *goot* stepmother. She is a devout woman. The children already know and like her."

"*Ja*, she is a *goot* woman." Karen's mind reeled. Nettie would become the woman of the house. She would run the home as she saw fit and Eli would support her decisions. Karen would have to step aside and give up the reins of control.

She would go from being the woman of the house back to being an unmarried daughter. In her community she was already seen as an old maid with few marriage prospects. All of her friends had married by twenty. Most had several children by the age of twenty-four.

"You are taking this very well." Her father smiled in relief and patted her knee.

"I want you to be happy, Papa."

"*Danki*. We have decided to wait until next fall. Nettie wants her children who live in Pennsylvania to be able to attend and one of her daughters there is expecting soon. I'm telling you this because I want you to start going to the singings again. You must look about for a husband of your own, Karen. Who knows, perhaps there will be more than one wedding in the family."

A husband of her own. As her father's words sank in, one name slipped into Karen's mind. John Doe.

Quickly, she dismissed the thought. Even without her responsibilities to the children and her father, she had made a vow before God and the community to uphold the ways of the Amish faith. Her first responsibility was always to God.

John was an outsider and forbidden. No matter how much she liked him she could never forget that fact.

Anna pursed her lips as she stared at John. "What is *haus?*"

John held back his grin. The kid was so serious. "House."

"*Haus-dach?*" Anna snapped quickly.

House something. He racked his brain until the answer popped into his head. "House roof."

"*Goot.* What is *natt?*"

"That is… Don't tell me. That is wet." Proud of himself, he smiled broadly.

"*Nee.* Wet is *nass. Natt* is north."

"North, *natt.* Wet, *nass.* Got it." Learning a new language wasn't easy. Especially when Karen was nearby to distract him.

"Handkerchief?"

His shoulders slumped. "You're making this too hard, Anna."

"We did this one yesterday." She gave him *that look.* The one that reminded him so much of Karen when one of the children stepped out of line.

He took his best guess. "Handkerchief is *shoeduck*."

"No, it's *shnubbe-duch*," Anna corrected in her most serious voice.

"Oh, come on. I was close."

Glancing to where Karen stood at the sink listening, John caught her smile at his wheedling. He didn't know what was more adorable, Anna as the benevolent and determined teacher or Karen as his amused and supportive audience.

For the past three days when Anna arrived home from school she quickly finished her chores and set up her classroom at the kitchen table. She called John in from work when she was ready. Their interchanges had become the highlight of his afternoons.

Anna said, "Now we're going to work on colors. What color is Karen's dress?"

He leaned back in his chair happy for the opportunity to study Karen openly. "That's difficult to say. Your sister's dress is sort of sea-foam green. Her apron is black, but her hair is honey-gold. Her lips are ruby-red and her eyes are the same beautiful sky-blue that you have, Anna."

Karen continued peeling potatoes. "And John is trying to avoid answering the question because he doesn't know the Amish word for green."

Busted. "Sadly, that is exactly what I'm trying to do. Anna, can we do the colors tomorrow? I have to go into town this afternoon. I've got a job interview."

Karen looked at him in surprise. "A job interview? Where?"

"Your father made arrangements with Reuben Beachy to give me a try. If I can do the job he'll take me on as an apprentice."

"The harness maker? That sounds like a fine job."

Without a driver's license or a social security card John was limited to where he could apply for work. The Amish carried neither of those trappings of the outside world. "Any job is a good thing because I need to be able to support myself. Your father has kindly loaned me the farm wagon to drive."

"Why don't you take the buggy?" Karen offered.

"Your *daed* is using it." John glanced at Anna to see if he'd gotten the word for father correct. She grinned and gave him a thumbs-up.

A puzzled expression appeared on Karen's features. "Where has Papa gone?"

"To see Nettie Sutter," Anna answered. "He's sweet on her."

"No kidding?" John looked to Karen for confirmation.

She nodded. "Anna, can you get me a jar of peaches from the cellar?"

When the child was out of the room, Karen turned to John. "My father and Nettie are to be married next fall. Please don't say anything to the children yet. He hasn't told them."

"Sure. Are you okay with your father getting remarried?"

Her chin came up. "Why wouldn't I be?"

"Won't it make some big changes for you?"

"I will have more help in the kitchen. I won't mind that." She didn't sound enthusiastic.

"What things will you mind?" he asked gently.

Laying her knife aside, she bowed her head. "I have raised them like my own children. Anna can barely remember our mother. Now I must step aside and let another woman take my place. How do I do that?"

Rising from the table, John walked to where she stood and rested his hands on her shoulders. "You have always done what is best for the children. You will continue to do that."

She tipped her head to the side and laid her cheek against his fingers. "You are right. The children must come first."

John's gesture of comfort quickly changed into something deeper. His need to hold her threatened to destroy his self-control. He could feel her slender collar bones beneath his hands, the softness of her cheek against his knuckles. His body ached with the effort it took not to slip his arms around her and pull her against him.

"*Danki,*" she breathed the word out and he knew she treasured his touch as much as he treasured her nearness.

The cellar door banged opened and Anna raced into the room with a jar of peaches in her hand. "Is one enough, sister?" she asked, setting the quart container on the table.

John quickly dropped his hands and stepped away, hoping the child hadn't noticed.

"*Ja,* one is fine." Karen picked up her knife and began peeling potatoes again.

John took hold of the jar. "Let me open this for you."

"I can manage," Karen turned to take it from him, but he shifted away.

"I've got it." He gritted his teeth as he tried to twist the lid and break the seal. It didn't budge.

"I have a jar opener if you need it," Karen offered, a smile twitching at the corner of her adorable lips.

"No." He grunted as he battled the tightest lid ever to grace a jar of produce. Karen folded her arms and waited. Anna giggled.

He held it below his waist to try a new angle. That did the trick. The ring gave way, he popped off the seal and in triumph, held the jar aloft. It slipped from his hand, struck the corner of the table and shattered, spilling peaches, glass shards and juice down his pant legs and across the floor boards.

In the ensuring stunned silence, Anna sighed and said, "I'll go get another jar, but John can't open this one."

Feeling his face heat to flaming red, he said to Karen, "I'm so sorry."

"Don't worry." Karen struggled to keep from laughing but lost the battle. Her delightful giggle gladdened his heart.

Suddenly, he was laughing, too. He spread his hands wide. "I got it open. What more do you want?"

She regained a modicum of composure, but giggles continued to slip out. "I didn't want them on the floor, John."

He looked down and saw a peach half had landed on the toe of his shoe. He raised his foot toward Karen. "This one is still good."

She broke into laughter and turned her face away. "Yuck."

Plucking the peach from his soaking shoe, he said, "Yuck. After my great display of strength all you can say is yuck? I'll show you yuck."

He made as if to press the fruit to her face. She squealed and ducked away, slipping around to the other side of the table.

"John, you wouldn't."

"Don't tempt me, woman." He advanced slowly. He was between her and the doorway. There was nowhere for her to run. That didn't stop her from trying. She darted past him, but he caught her and backed her into the wall. With her laughter still ringing in his ears, he touched the peach to the tip of her nose.

"John!" She rubbed her nose vigorously on her sleeve. The laughter died in his throat as he realized he had her exactly where he wanted her. In his arms. Close to his heart.

She met his gaze and the smile faded from her face, too. Her lips were so close. All he had to do was bend down a little. When he did, she turned her face away. With her arms braced against his chest, she said, "Please, don't."

She might as well have asked him to stop breathing. But for her—he would do even that.

Karen heard the sound of Anna's footsteps coming up the stairs over the drumming of her pulse. Staring into John's eyes, Karen saw the same intense longing there that was racing through her blood. Her heart yearned to answer his unspoken request, but she could not.

His expression went carefully blank. Dropping his arms from around her, he stepped back and said, "I'll help clean up."

Anna came into the room and set the second jar on the cabinet. "I'm not going to fetch another one."

Karen moved away from John, keeping her gaze averted but she could feel him watching her every move. "I can manage. John, you need to get changed for your job interview unless you want to go smelling like peaches."

He looked down at his pants. "These are my only jeans."

Anna's mouth opened in shock. "You've been wearing the same pair of jeans every day for a month?"

He was quick to defend himself. "Hey, I wash them. They dry pretty quick in front of the fire but they won't get dry before I have to see Mr. Beachy today."

"I have some clothes you can borrow." Karen's thundering heart slowed painfully. She couldn't take much more of this.

Anna said, "Papa's clothes will be too big on him."

"I know. I have some of Seth's things in a cedar chest. I think they will fit. I'll go get them."

"If you're sure you don't mind." John watched her closely. He always sought to make sure she was okay. She admired that about him.

"I do not mind, John Doe, but I thank you for

your concern. It is *goot* that some use can be made of them."

He spread his arms wide. "Okay. I will take care of this while you do that."

His eagerness to help was another thing she found endearing about him. Quickly she climbed the stairs to the attic and opened a large flat trunk in the center of the room. The clothes lay where she had put them the day after the funerals. Her mother's dresses and shoes and her songbook lay on top. Beneath it her sisters' aprons, handkerchiefs and *kapps* were neatly folded. To one side was Seth's dark suit and his black hat stuffed with paper to keep its shape.

Karen sank to her knees beside the trunk. She hadn't been up here in over a year. As much as she loved and missed the members of her family, life went on.

Pulling Seth's clothes from the trunk, Karen closed the lid and walked down the stairs. John and Anna were emptying the last of the broken glass into the trash can. The floor had been swept and washed.

Forcing a smile to her face, Karen approached John and handed him the bundle. "Try these on, I think they might fit."

"Thank you." He accepted the clothes from her.

"It's *danki,* John," Anna corrected.

"Danki, teetshah." He bowed in her direction and she beamed.

When he went out the door Karen clung to the soft glow he left behind. Never in her wildest dream had she thought she would fall for an outsider. In spite of all her resolutions and prayers, she was falling hard for John Doe.

John changed into the plain clothes with mixed feelings. Once again Karen had come to his rescue. Was it possible his affection for her was nothing more than misguided gratitude? She had been there for him at every turn.

No, he didn't believe it. Maybe he didn't remember what loving someone felt like, but being near Karen felt like love.

The trousers were a little big at the waist and the cuffs fell over the top of his shoes. They would need to be shortened, but they would do for today. The shirt was a better fit. He searched for belt loops and found none. He clipped on the suspenders and raised them over his shoulders but they didn't feel right. In his mind old men wore suspenders.

Maybe it just felt odd wearing another man's clothes.

After pulling on the jacket John stared at the black felt hat lying on the table. The hat was the crowning touch. It, more than anything else, would make him appear Amish. Should he wear it? What would Karen think? Would she like him better in plain clothing?

Sighing, he hung the hat on a wooden peg by the front door. He didn't want to pretend he was something he wasn't.

Stepping outside the grandfather house John brushed at the creases in the coat. Summoning his courage he walked to the main house front door and entered. Karen was rolling out pie dough on the kitchen counter. She turned around to study him with a flour-covered rolling pin in one hand. There was a smudge of flour on her cheek. His hand itched to brush it away but he knew such attention would be unwelcome. Anna was nowhere in sight.

"What's the verdict?" Spreading his arms wide, he turned around slowly.

"You look Plain, John Doe."

Dropping his arms, he tucked his hands in the pockets of his trousers. "Who knows, maybe I am. Would that make a difference to you?"

She turned back to the table and resumed rolling the dough. "I don't think you are Amish. You don't know the language, you don't know our ways."

He took a step closer, not understanding why he needed to push the issue. "But if I were Amish, would that make things right between us?"

She paused. "*Nee*. It would not."

"Why?"

Facing him, a gentle expression filled her eyes. "You cling to me because you know no one else."

Was she right? Hadn't that very thought crossed his mind only a few minutes before? He refused to accept it. "You make me sound like a child, Karen. I'm not."

"Give yourself more time, John. Your answers may yet come to you."

"Okay, that's fair. But you should know something. How I feel about you isn't going to change no matter what I discover about myself."

Spinning on his heels, he headed out the door. He had a job interview to get to. He had to start building some kind of life for himself. He wasn't clinging to Karen because she was the only woman in his life. He had to prove that to her.

He would get a place of his own, live in the community, make friends among them. Eventually, he would become one of them.

Was such a thing possible? He wasn't sure.

If it was, he would do it. Then Karen would see his feelings were genuine.

He was crossing toward the barn when the sound of a car reached him. As he watched, Sheriff Bradley drove into the snow-covered yard.

Chapter Twelve

The tires of the sheriff's SUV crunched loudly on the crisp snow as he pulled to a stop beside John. Opening the vehicle door, Nick stepped out. "Afternoon, John."

John dipped his head. "Sheriff. What brings you out here?"

"Not good news I'm afraid. I wanted to let you know we got a report back from the FBI on your DNA and fingerprints. You're not in their system."

John's last bit of hope crumpled like a wadded piece of paper. He was no better and no worse off than he'd been five minutes ago. He still had a plan. He still needed to get to his job interview. "Thanks for the update, Nick."

"I'm sorry it wasn't better news."

John's gaze was drawn to the house. "I guess that means I'm stuck here."

"My offer of a place to stay in Millersburg still stands, John. I think you'd be better off in town."

"I appreciate that, but I'm doing okay."

"On an Amish farm? Look, I've got nothing against the Amish, I've got family who are Amish, but why cut yourself off from contact with the outside world? I mean, who knows, maybe you'll see something on the six-o'clock news that sparks a memory about a place or someone you know. You're insulated here, John. That may make remembering even harder."

"Maybe, maybe not." John crossed his arms over his chest.

"Suit yourself, but you might want to be asking yourself why you're hiding out here."

Staring at his boots, John pushed a clump of snow aside with his toe. "For one thing, someone tried to kill me. You haven't a clue who that was. I think I'm safer here than I would be on the streets of a city."

"You're probably right about that."

Looking at the sheriff, John said, "Thanks for your concern. If anything new comes up you know where to find me."

"All right. I just wanted you to know that I'm not giving up. I'm going to keep digging."

"I'm not giving up hope either, but there comes a point when I have to move on. I've read dozens of stories about people who've been missing for decades. I've even read about people like me. People who never recover their memory. I have to prepare myself for that possibility."

To his surprise, John got the job with Reuben Beachy at the harness shop. His success had more to do with Reuben's outright curiosity about John's condition than John's skill with the tools of a harness maker's trade.

The spry, elderly Amishman whistled or hummed continually while he worked on his large pedal-operated sewing machine. John's job was to take orders over the phone and from customers as well as cutting lengths of leather or synthetic biothane into the sizes his boss needed.

Reuben, as it turned out, had been making harnesses for more than sixty years. He made gear for everything from mini to draft-size horses. Recently, he had added leather dog collars and leashes to his inventory. Most of those he sold to dealers out of state.

Chuckling, Reuben confided to John on his first day at work, "A product with 'Amish Made' guarantees it is of *goot* quality and 'green' because we make it without the use of electricity. The English like that now. Once we were seen as backward people, but now they think we are on to something. It always makes me laugh."

It wasn't the only thing that made Reuben laugh. Every day he regaled John with witty comments and funny stories. Having seen the more serious side of the Amish, John was happy to see that humor had a place in the tight-knit community. By the end of his first week at work, John realized he had made a genuine friend.

Leaving a customer at the front counter, John entered the work area and approached the oversize sewing machine where the gnomelike bearded man toiled. "Reuben, David Miller is here to pick up a new harness he ordered."

Reuben stopped pedaling. "Would that be Pudgy Dave Miller or Smokey Dave Miller?"

"I've got no idea. How would I tell?" The man was a lean muscular farmer.

Ruben cackled. "Ach, we have so many people with the same names around here that we need nicknames to tell them apart. Pudgy Dave has blond hair. He isn't pudgy now, but he sure was when he was a boy."

"Then it must be Smokey Dave out front because his hair is brown."

Rubin rose from his seat and moved to where several large boxes were stacked on a bench. Selecting one, he handed it to John. "This should be it."

"Are you going to tell me how Smokey Dave got his name?"

"His house caught on fire. They saved the place, but he got a nickname real quick."

"I guess that makes sense." John took the box to the waiting customer, collected the money then turned over the closed sign.

Reuben was putting away his supplies when John returned to the room. As he was clearing away the leather scraps, Reuben said, "My mother's name was Miriam. What was your mother called?"

John waited for something to pop into his mind but nothing did. Finally, he shrugged. "I don't know. I don't remember."

"Which way is Texas from here?"

"Southwest," John answered without hesitation.

"Ever been there?"

"I don't know. Are we going to play Twenty Questions every night when we close up?"

"This is a strange illness you have, John Doe."

"No kidding."

"I know a good faith healer if you want to try one. I know you English don't set much store by that kind of thing, but Elmer Hertzler has a way with herbs."

"I'm coming to accept the fact that I may not remember more than snatches of my previous life."

"If that is what God wills, it is good that you should accept it."

"Reuben, what does it take to become Amish?"

Chuckling, Reuben winked. "An Amish *mamm* and *daed*."

"All joking aside, can an outsider join the Amish church?"

"It has been done, but not by many. The ones I know who have tried have all left within a few months."

That wasn't what John wanted to hear.

Reuben sensed his disappointment. "If you admire our devotion to God, John Doe, be more devout in your own life. You don't need a black hat for that. If you think our plain, frugal ways are good, become plain and frugal in your life. We do not live fairy-tale lives as the English make us sound."

"I know that. I'm trying to be devout. I'm living plain, but I believe the Amish faith is the life for me."

Reuben stroked his long gray beard. "You are serious."

"I am. I think God placed me here for a reason."

Suddenly, Reuben started chuckling again. "You mean you've fallen for an Amish girl. That's the usual reason a man starts asking questions about our religion."

John felt searing heat rush to his face. "That may be part of it, but it's not the only reason I'm interested in learning more about the Amish faith."

Reuben wagged a finger at him. "Just remember, Adam had it pretty good in Eden until he started listening to a woman."

"They can't be all bad. You're married."

"*Ja*, three times. I maybe should have quit at two." He began chuckling again. "Don't tell my Martha I said that."

John smiled. "I won't. Three times? I thought the Amish weren't allowed to divorce and remarry."

"We are not. My first wife died in childbirth a year after our wedding. My second wife took sick and died from cancer. That was a hard time for me. Martha lost her husband to a stroke about the same time. Two years later we wed. I thought we had a lot in common, but it seems we didn't. If you are serious about becoming one of us you will need to learn the language and live among us for a time."

"For how long?"

"The English, always in a rush. Until you are accepted as one of us. It make take a year or it may take five years."

John quelled his need to rush forward into this

new life. He wanted, needed, to belong somewhere. "Anna Imhoff is teaching me the language."

"Good. I can help with that, too. You should speak to Bishop Zook. He is the man who could help guide you."

John hesitated. Would it cause trouble for Karen if her bishop knew an outsider was interested in courting her? It wasn't that they had done anything wrong, but with John living on her farm it could give that impression. "Thanks, Reuben. I'll think on it."

"Pray about it, John Doe. God's wisdom is far beyond our own understanding. Now come, it's payday for you." Reuben led the way to the cash drawer and began counting out John's wages for the week.

Happy to have money that he'd earned himself, John pocketed the bills. After hitching one of Eli's horses to his borrowed cart, John swung by the grocery store on his way home. Leaving his horse at one of the hitching rails at the front of the store, John noticed Molly dozing at the next rail down.

Inside the store, he quickly spied Karen. Now that he left early for work each day and spent his free time working with Eli's horses, John saw her only at breakfast and for an hour or so in the evenings after supper. Normally her family surrounded her but today it appeared that she was alone.

Taking a cart from the line by the doorway he pushed it in her direction. Her eyes brightened when she caught sight of him.

He counted out several bills and offered them to her. "You're just the person I wanted to see. I'd like you to take this."

She placed two sacks of sugar in her cart. "What is that for?"

"You do all my cooking. I feel I should contribute more than just my rent."

"Especially after you got my father to lower it?" she suggested.

"Okay, yes."

"Very well." She extended her hand.

He made a sad face at his money. "Goodbye, hard-earned cash. When you go into Karen's pocket I know I'll not see you again."

She struggled not to smile at his teasing. Snatching the money from him, she said, "*Ja*, when money goes into my pocket it does not come out easily."

"So I've heard."

"Are you liking your new job?"

"I do. Reuben is a fine man to work for. It tickles him that I can't remember things. He's worse than Anna and Noah combined, with all his questions."

Karen chuckled. "I see you are wearing your plain clothes." She had given John several pairs of shortened pants as well as a couple of shirts. They went a long way toward stretching his meager wardrobe. He no longer had to spend the evenings wrapped in a quilt at home while his jeans dried over a chair in front of the stove.

John leaned on his cart as Karen piled several large bags of flour in her cart followed by two big cans of shortening. He said, "Reuben's going to help me with my Amish, too. Don't tell Anna. I want her to think I'm improving because of her teaching."

A slight smile curved Karen's lips. "I won't breathe a word."

It was nice talking about ordinary things, walking beside Karen, doing a simple thing like shopping. "Anna's really excited about her Christmas program. She keeps asking me if I remember that I said I would come."

"It is the one time that Amish children are encouraged to perform. Although we strive to remain humble before God and the world, you will see many proud parents and grandparents in the audience. And you will enjoy the entire program as most of it is in English."

"That's a relief. My Pennsylvania Dutch isn't progressing very fast."

"*Nee.* Do not disparage yourself. You are doing well."

She had noticed. His spirits lightened. "I was wondering what kind of Christmas presents would be appropriate for me to get the children?"

"Only little things."

"Define little things for me because an iPod is a little thing and I'm pretty sure that's not what you're thinking of."

"Colored pencils for Anna. A board game for Noah. Things like that. Homemade gifts are best."

John couldn't think of any simple thing he could make or buy that would be appropriate to give Karen. Perhaps Reuben could give him some ideas.

He said, "Okay, that's a start. Tell me what an Amish Christmas is like. Will you get a tree or decorate?"

"*Nee,* we do not allow ourselves to be distracted from the meaning of the day by such commercial things. We put up some greenery in the house, but Christmas Day is for reflecting about our Lord's birth. We will have family and friends over or we will travel to visit others. We do much visiting this time of year."

He hadn't considered he might be spending Christmas alone. The thought was utterly depressing. He strived to sound casual when he asked, "What are your plans for this year?"

"Nettie, Elam and Katie will have dinner with us on Christmas Day. Some of our cousins are coming, too. It will be fun. On second Christmas we will be traveling to visit some of my mother's family in Pennsylvania for a few days."

"What's second Christmas?"

"The twenty-sixth. It's when we exchange gifts. Goodness, I have so much baking to get done before then." She perked up and pushed her cart down the aisle.

John drew back to let another shopper past, then he stepped up beside Karen again. She was comparing the prices of poppy-seed filling on two brands. John asked, "What kind of gift would your father like?"

"Save your money, John," she chided. "You do not need to get gifts for our family."

"Yes…*ja,* I do."

She pressed her hand to her lips to hold back a giggle without success.

"What?" he demanded.

"It seems funny that you want to be like us."

"Your family, the Amish lifestyle, it's really all I know."

Sadness clouded her bright eyes. "A hen may sit on a duck's egg until it hatches, but the baby will still be a duckling and not a chick."

"I'm not a hapless egg. I have a choice about how I want to live my life. God has given me that. I don't know what I was in the past, but I know what I want in my future."

"And what is that?" she asked quietly.

"You."

As she stared at him in openmouthed shock, he smiled at her then rounded the corner of the aisle, picked up the things he'd stopped for and went to check out.

That evening Karen kept her composure through supper and the rest of the evening, but when John announced he was going to turn in she made an excuse to follow him a few minutes later.

He waited for her outside. She raised her shawl over her hair against the chill night air. A sliver of moon low in the west illuminated the nighttime farm. The combination of moonlight on snow gave her just enough light to see John's face.

Suddenly, she was beset with doubts. Had she misunderstood him earlier today? She had been so shocked by his words that she hadn't been able to demand an explanation. The moonlit setting and her racing heart were making it difficult to broach the subject.

"Is there something you need, Karen?"

The hint of humor in his voice pushed aside her reservations. If he had been toying with her she wasn't amused. "You can't make a statement like you did in the store and then walk away without an explanation."

"You mean when I said I wanted you in my future? I truly meant that."

There it was again, that softness in his tone that made her knees weak and sent the blood humming through her veins. She folded her arms tightly across her chest and walked away from the house. John fell into step beside her.

A dozen thoughts warred inside her brain. She cared for John so much, but her love of God and her family could not be brushed aside easily. She hardened her heart against the hurt she was about to cause him.

He was close beside her, but not touching her. They left the yard and walked side by side down the lane. The snow-covered fields reflected the moonlight with a gray-white glow. Overhead, the stars sparkled in the inky blackness. The whole world lay hushed except for the crunch of their footsteps on the frosty snow.

Finally, she said, "What you want is not possible, John."

"Because I am not Amish?"

"Yes."

"What if I became Amish? What if I joined your faith? Would there be a chance for us, then?"

"Why would you do this?"

"Because God brought me to this place for a reason. All around me are simple hardworking people who devote every day to the glory of God. Surly you don't think I'm here by chance?"

"I do not."

"You and your family have shown me that religion isn't about Sunday services. It's about doing what God has instructed us to do in the Bible. I'm serious, Karen. I want to embrace a new life. I can do that here. It feels right. If you are the woman who can help me do that, then I will be doubly blessed."

She stopped and faced him. His gaze, intense and piercing, never wavered. Was it possible he could join her faith? It wouldn't be easy. What if he did manage to do it and then his memory came back to him? Would he want to stay? There was no way to be certain.

"What are you asking of me, John?"

"For now, acceptance is all I ask."

No promises, no bold talk of overpowering love. She pondered what he asked and realized it was something she could do. "All right. I accept that you have a strong desire to learn about my faith and to become one of us."

"Thank you. How do you think your family will feel about it?"

After a second, she shook her head. "Skeptical."

"I can always trust you to tell me the truth."

Karen knew that wasn't true. If it were, she would be telling him how firmly he was planted in her heart and mind and how much she longed to find a way to be with him in every sense. Yet a prickle of doubt about his motives could not be silenced by her own desires.

It had only been a month and a half since she found him on the road. It was too soon. It was too soon to know her own heart and too soon for him to know his.

He tipped his head toward the house. "We should get back. I don't want you to get sick, with Christmas less than three weeks away."

"*Ja,* I have much to do." And much to think about.

On Saturday, John went out to continue working with the horses. He was surprised but happy to find Jacob waiting inside the barn to help him. John was grateful for a chance to spend some one-on-one time with the lad.

Together they continued training Jenny and One-Way. By now, both young horses accepted their harnesses without a problem and could be hitched and unhitched from a cart and driven short distances. The young filly proved more temperamental than the colt, but both of them were progressing well.

After putting One-Way through his paces out on

a narrow dirt-packed road that circled the inside of the pasture, John drove him back to the barn where Jacob waited to take Jenny out next. John drew the colt to a halt and looked at Jacob. "What do you think about taking this fellow out on the highway?"

Looking pleased to have his opinion consulted, Jacob said, "He's spent plenty of time tethered near the road to get used to traffic. It doesn't seem to bother him anymore. *Ja,* I think he is ready."

John offered the reins. "Would you mind driving him? You've got more experience and more skill than I do. I've worn him out this morning. I think he'll behave, but I'd like to ride along to see how he does."

Jacob's slender chest puffed out at the compliment. He quickly climbed into the two-wheeled cart beside John and turned the horse around. John jumped out to open the gate and close it behind them, then resumed his seat.

In the front yard a buggy sat in front of the barn. Through the open door John saw Eli wearing a heavy leather apron as he examined the hoof of a palomino pony. Reuben Beachy stood beside Eli watching him work. He caught sight of John and waved. John waved back, happy to know he had at least one friend outside of the Imhoff family.

John asked Jacob, "When did your father start shoeing horses again?"

"He announced last night that he thought his arm was strong enough to try it."

"I'm glad for him."

"*Ja*, he has missed it."

"Do you plan to be a farrier, too?"

"Maybe. I'm strong enough." Jacob scowled at John, daring him to disagree.

"I think a man can do anything he puts his mind to. It isn't always about being the strongest."

"Karen thinks I can't do it," Jacob admitted.

"Karen worries about you, that's all. She will come around if that is what you really want to do."

"Maybe." The boy's tone carried a heavy dose of doubt. Before John could explore the subject further, they reached the highway. Since it was Saturday, John knew there would be less traffic on the road, but he still wasn't sure how One-Way would handle the new situation.

The horse took to the roadway as if he'd been doing it all his life. Even a passing car didn't disturb him.

John said, "It seems he has inherited his mother's calm nature as well as his father's speed. It's a good combination. Someone is going to be very happy with this colt."

Jacob urged the horse to pick up his pace. "I'd love to see how fast he can go."

John laid a hand on the boy's arm. "Me, too, but this isn't the time or place for it."

The boy shot John a sour look but pulled the horse back. After two miles, John said, "I think this is good. Let's take him home."

As they slowed to turn around, an open buggy drawn by a high-stepping trotter came down the road, and One-Way whinnied a greeting. The Amish teenager driving the other vehicle drew to a halt.

"*Guder mariye,* Jacob," he called out.

"Hello, Henry." Jacob replied brightly. It was easy to read the hero-worship on his face.

John recognized the young man as one of Bishop Zook's sons. He'd seen Jacob hanging out with him and several older boys at the wedding and in town after school.

"Is this Eli's racehorse I've been hearing about?" Henry cast a critical eye over the colt.

"*Ja,* it is." Jacob couldn't disguise the pride in his voice.

Henry turned his attention to John. "Are you the *dummkopf*—the *Englischer* who can't remember his own name?

Chapter Thirteen

The teenager's mocking tone caught John completely by surprise. He'd met with nothing but sympathy and kindness among the Amish. He was unprepared for ridicule.

Henry's smile turned snide. "Your horse doesn't look all that fast, Jacob. I think my Dobby could beat him running on three legs."

Jacob rose to the challenge. "I don't think so."

"Too bad we can't find out." With a laugh, Henry slapped his lines hard on the back of his sweaty horse and headed down the road at a breakneck pace.

John said, "Your friend isn't a very good judge of horseflesh." He wasn't kind, either.

Urging One-Way toward home, Jacob said, "Henry was just kidding."

John didn't believe that for a minute. "Is Henry a good friend of yours?"

"Sure. I'm his buddy."

"He seems quite a bit older than you."

"Henry is eighteen, but he doesn't mind if I hang out with him. He knows how to have fun. He has a swell radio in his buggy."

"I thought listening to the radio was frowned upon as worldly."

"Just because a bunch of old geezers don't like modern music that doesn't make it wrong. Besides, we are in our *rumspringa*. We get to do those kinds of things."

"Aren't you too young for your *rumspringa?*"

"Henry says I'm not."

"He likes to race, doesn't he?"

"Sometimes." John could feel Jacob's retreat.

The whole situation didn't sit well with John, but what could he do? He was finally making some headway in getting to know Jacob. If he told Karen or Eli his vague suspicions that Jacob was involved in illicit buggy racing he would be guilty of betraying the boy's confidences.

What choice did that leave him? The only thing he could do was keep a watchful eye on Jacob.

On Sunday morning John joined the family in the buggy as they were getting ready to leave for church services. He looked forward to the day although it was barely six o'clock. The service would be at the home of a family some fifteen miles away. Eli had gone ahead with the bench wagon a half hour earlier.

John squeezed into the backseat between Noah and Jacob. Karen rode up front with Anna. When they were on their way, John found the courage to ask, "What can I expect today?"

"To be bored stiff," Jacob answered under his breath.

A sharp look from Karen proved he'd been overheard. She said, "Worship begins at about eight o'clock and it usually lasts until after eleven. Women are seated in one area, and men in another."

"Three hours on a backless bench?" John winced. What had he gotten himself into?

Karen continued. "Hymns are sung from the *Ausbund,* a special hymnal used by us. The songs were written by martyrs for our faith over four hundred years ago."

"So, no English songs I can sing along with?"

"*Nee.* There will be two preachers along with Bishop Zook at the service. They will take turns preaching. The first sermon begins about eight-thirty. It will be in Pennsylvania Dutch. Scriptures are read in High German. Did you bring your English Bible so you can follow along?"

He patted his coat pocket. "Yes, I did."

The trip was long and tiring, and everyone was glad to get out when they finally arrived at the

service site. A group of men in charge of unhitching the buggies and taking the horses into the barn
quickly went to work to settle Molly after her long
trip.

John felt awkward joining the men as they
began to file into the house, but Eli was there
already and Reuben came over to quickly make
John feel welcome. A long row of black hats lined
the porch wall. John added his to the end and took
a moment to wonder how he would find it again
out of the seventy or so hanging there.

Noah tugged John's coat. "Don't worry, I'll poke
you if you start to fall asleep."

"Gee, thanks."

The benches were as hard as John feared, but
when the hymns began he was mesmerized by
the simple beauty and power of the singing. There
was no organ or musical instrument of any kind.
The profoundly moving and mournful sound was
created by more than a hundred people packed
into the lower rooms of the house.

He couldn't follow the preaching, but he read
and studied the passages Eli pointed out to him. In
his own way he felt connected to the outpouring
of faith around him.

After an hour, he felt Noah slump against him.
Looking down, he saw the boy had nodded off.
He wasn't the only one. At least one of the very
elderly men who had been given household chairs

to sit in was snoring softly. John nudged Noah who quickly sat up straight, but no one bothered the elder in the corner.

When the meeting came to an end, John closed his book, feeling refreshed in mind and body. Had he felt like this before during a church service? Had he known this closeness to God and lost it?

He glanced across the room and caught sight of Karen. Had he known this special closeness with a woman and forgotten it?

"Our program is tonight. It's tonight. It's tonight. I can't wait. I can't wait." Anna's excitement had been growing by leaps and bounds over the past days. Tonight was finally Christmas Eve and her school program was only an hour away.

Anna hopped around the kitchen table repeating her refrain until Karen finally had enough.

"Silence, little sister."

Anna immediately stopped chanting but continued to bounce. Karen tried not to smile and took pity on her. She remembered well her own anticipation for the biggest night of the school year.

"Why don't you go see if John is back," Karen suggested hoping for a moment of peace and quiet to finish her preparations. There were fresh cookies cooling on the rack that would have to be packed for the trip and her peanut brittle was nearly done. She couldn't stop stirring for fear it would scorch.

But peace and quiet was not to be hers. Before Anna reached the front door, it opened and John stepped into the room.

Anna grabbed his hand. *"Frehlicher-Grischtdaag,* John. I knew you wouldn't forget."

"Merry Christmas to you, too. It's your big night. How could I forget that? Reuben had us close the shop early so I could get home in time to go with you."

He was wearing his plain clothes and her brother's hat. Karen's heart expanded with happiness. Knowing that John was seeking God and a place in her community warmed her inside and out. If only she dare believe such a thing was possible.

She glanced at the clock. It was a few minutes after one o'clock in the afternoon. "Anna, go tell your father it's time to get ready."

The child rocketed out of the house without bothering to put on her coat. John chuckled. "She's ready to pop with excitement."

"She is. Noah is almost as bad. The children spend weeks, even months, making preparations for their Christmas program. They'll sing songs, read poems, as if you hadn't already learned that from Anna, and they will have a play about the meaning of Christmas. It's a big deal for them."

"It sounds like a lot of fun. What can I do to help you get ready?"

"Stack those cookies in these plastic containers and don't snitch. They are for the children's teacher." She motioned with her hand toward the container.

"You never let me have any fun. How do you know they are any good? I should test them." He popped one in his mouth.

"John!"

"They're fine," he mumbled around his full mouth. He packed the box to the brim and then snapped the lid in place. "Is there anything else I can test for you?"

Karen shook her head and returned to stirring her candy but her lighthearted mood persisted. He could always make her smile.

"Are you sure it's okay for me to come to this program?" he asked.

"*Ja*, there will be many English visitors. Lots of our families work for non-Amish businesses and have non-Amish friends. We welcome them to share the joy of Christ's birth."

Noah and Jacob came through the front door. Noah shook off his hat. "It's snowing again. Papa says we should take the sleigh."

Anna came in behind them wrapped in her father's big coat. "We're going to have a sleigh ride!"

Eli, smiling indulgently at his littlest daughter, closed the door behind her.

Only Karen looked upset at the prospect. "Really, Papa? Can't we take the buggy? It will be so much warmer."

"*Nee*, the snow is piling up fast. You won't think it's warmer if you must walk home and leave the buggy stuck in a drift."

"Very well. Jacob, Noah, get the lap robes from the chest upstairs. Everyone else, go get dressed or we will be late."

Everyone departed. Only John remained in the kitchen. Karen began carefully pouring her hot peanut-brittle candy over the nuts arranged on wax paper in a long pan.

"Are you sure I can't test that for you?" John's voice tickled her ear. He stood close behind her. Suddenly, her hands began to shake. Quickly, he grasped the pan handle enclosing her fingers beneath his own to help steady it. "Careful."

Trying to ignore the rush of emotions singing through her heart, she said, "There is nothing for you to test here. It's too hot."

"But I have a sweet tooth."

"Your sweet tooth will have to wait."

"Can't. This will have to tide me over." He planted a quick kiss on her cheek.

She should scold him, but the words died in her

throat. Instead, she cast a sly grin his way. "Go harness Benny to the sleigh and be quick about it."

"Yes, ma'am." He winked at her as he went out the door.

Returning to her work, Karen began humming her favorite Christmas song.

John didn't waste any time getting the big draft horse hitched. Within ten minutes he was waiting outside the front door for the rest of the family. For some reason he was almost as excited as Anna. A sleigh ride with Karen beside him was his idea of the perfect romantic Christmas Eve.

Anna was the first one out of the house. She quickly claimed her spot in the front seat. Noah scrambled up beside her with the lap robes in his arms. John gave over the reins and took his place in the back. Noah handed several robes to John then spread one over himself and Anna. Wiggles and giggles was the only way John could think to describe Anna's demeanor.

Karen and Eli came next carrying boxes filled with treats that they stowed on the floor. "Everyone be careful not to step on these," Karen cautioned with a pointed look in John's direction.

Eli took his place up front and that left Karen standing beside the sleigh with no choice but to sit next to John. He smiled broadly and patted the seat.

After casting a quick glance at her father, she got in. John spread the robe over her and said in a low voice, "Don't worry. I won't let you freeze."

"Jacob! Come on," Anna shouted, causing the patient horse to toss his head.

Jacob came out the door letting it slam shut behind him. He had been trying to act as if the program was no big deal, but John could see he was excited, too. The teenager piled in the back-seat with them.

After a second or two of getting settled, Jacob said, "Scoot over, Karen, and give me some room."

John grinned. *Thank you, Jacob.*

Wishing he could give the boy a pat on the back, John lifted his arm to make more room for Karen and laid it along the back of the seat. She moved closer, but remained stiff as a chunk of wood beside him. As much as he wanted to slip his arm around her shoulder, he knew it would only make her more uncomfortable.

"Ready, everyone?" Eli asked. Five confirmations rang out. Eli slapped the lines and the big horse took off down the snow-covered lane.

Sleigh bells jingled merrily in time with Benny's footfalls. The runners hissed along over the snow as big flakes continued to float down. They stuck to the hats of the men turning their brims white before long.

As Anna and Noah tried to catch snowflakes on their tongues between giggles, John leaned down to see Karen's face. "Are you warm enough?"

She nodded, but her face looked rosy and cold. John took off his woolen scarf and wrapped it around her head to cover her mouth and nose. "

"Thank you," she murmured.

"My pleasure. It's a perfect day, isn't it?"

The thick snow obscured the horizon and made the farm seem like the inside of a snow globe. The fields lay hidden under a thick blanket of white. Cedar tree branches drooped beneath their load of the white stuff. A hushed stillness filled the air broken only by the jingle of the harness bells. It was a picture-perfect moment in time.

The school lay only two miles from the farm. For John, they reached their destination all too soon. As they drew close they saw a dozen buggies and sleighs parked along the south side of the white wooden school building. All the horses had their faces close to the wall to keep them sheltered from the wind.

As everyone scrambled out of the sleigh, John offered Karen his hand to help her out. When she took it, he gave her an affectionate squeeze. She graced him with a shy smile in return.

Inside the building, the place was already

crowded with people. Student desks had been pushed out of the way to make room for benches down the center facing a small stage at the front of the room. Swags of fragrant cedar boughs decorated the windowsills and colorful paper chains ran from each corner to a light fixture in the center of the ceiling. Pegs along one wall held coats and hats while a table on the opposite wall bore trays of cookies and candies.

An atmosphere of joy, goodwill and anticipation permeated the air. Everywhere John looked there were welcoming smiles. The Imhoff children hurried to join their classmates behind a large screen off to one side of the stage. Eli, John and Karen found seats in the center.

For the next hour the little school became suspended in time. John saw parents and grandparents, aunts and uncles, friends and neighbors focused not on the problems of the world or their own lives, but on the stage where children preformed their assigned roles, not perfectly, but beautifully nonetheless.

Together the community shook with shared laughter and sighed with quiet joy as the reason for the season was retold not by preachers but by eager young voices. When the last song began, Jacob had a small solo. To John's surprise, the boy had a beautiful voice, by far the best in the group. His rendition of "Silent Night" was enough to bring tears to many eyes.

After the performance ended, Reuben Beachy came from the back of the school carrying a large sack. He didn't wear a red suit, but his beard was white and his eyes held a distinct twinkle as he preformed the role of Father Christmas and passed out small gifts to the children.

Anna was delighted with her gift, a wooden puzzle. The little girl beside her unwrapped a book. Although she tried to hide it, it was clear she wasn't as pleased with her gift. Noticing her friend's unhappiness, Anna offered to swap gifts.

John glanced at Karen. She had seen her little sister's unselfish act, and he knew she was pleased by it.

Later, when everyone had a plate of treats, Anna squeezed in between Karen and John. He said, "You did very well, Miss Anna. Your poem was perfection."

"Danki." Her excited high was fading.

"It was very nice of you to change gifts with your friend," Karen added.

Anna shrugged. "Mary already has that book. I don't."

"It was a *goot* thing anyway." Karen slipped her arm around the child and gave her a hug.

It was dark by the time the festivities wound

down and families began leaving. John brushed the accumulated snow from the sleigh's seats while Eli lit the lanterns on the sides. Benny stood quietly, one hip cocked and a dusting of snow across his back.

John stepped back inside to tell Karen they were ready. Scanning the room, he saw her with a group of young women. Two of them held babies on their hips. Karen raised a hand to smooth the blond curls of a little boy. As she did, her gaze met John's across the room. In that moment, he knew exactly what he wanted.

He wanted Karen to have the life she was meant to live and he wanted to be a part of it. He wanted to spend every Christmas with her for the rest of his life.

"Is it time to go home? I'm tired." Anna, sitting at her desk, could barely keep her eyes open.

"Yes, it's time to go home." He picked her up and she draped herself over his shoulder. Karen joined them a minute later.

In the sleigh, Noah and Jacob sat up front with their father leaving John to settle in with Anna across his lap and Karen seated beside him. The snow had stopped and a pale moon slipped in and out of the clouds as the horse made its way home. Snuggled beneath a blanket with Karen at his side, John marveled at the beauty of the winter night and the beauty of the woman next to him.

When they pulled up in front of the house, John handed Anna over to Eli, who carried her inside. The boys took the horse to the barn leaving John standing on the porch steps with Karen.

He said, "I had a wonderful time. Thank you for inviting me."

"I'm glad." She didn't seem eager to get in out of the cold.

"I had no idea an Amish Christmas could be so much fun." Or that it would clearly show him his heart's desire.

She said, "We are just getting started, John. Tomorrow we will have many guests for dinner. We will have games to play and stories to share."

He stepped closer. She fell silent but didn't move away. Reaching out, he cupped her cheek. "Merry Christmas, Karen."

"Merry Christmas to you, John." Her voice was a soft whisper in the night.

Slowly, he lowered his lips to hers and kissed her.

Chapter Fourteen

Karen knew she should turn away from John, but she couldn't make her body obey. His mouth closed over hers with incredible softness, a featherlight touch that wasn't enough.

She raised her face to him, and he deepened the kiss. A profound joy clutched her heart and stole her breath. This was the moment she had been waiting a lifetime to experience.

Her arms crept up to circle his neck and she drew him closer still. The sweet softness of his lips moved across her cheek, touched her eyelid and then her brow as if claiming every part of her. When he pulled away, Karen knew he owned a piece of her soul forever. She would never be the same.

His eyes roved across her face. "I love you, Karen. If I have to spend a lifetime proving it to you, I will."

Looking up at his beloved face, she whispered, "I do not doubt it for I love you, too."

Slipping his arms around her, he pulled her close. She leaned against his chest, feeling his strength and his tenderness as he held her. Nothing had ever felt this right and yet she knew it was wrong.

With his cheek resting against her hair, he said, "You've taken the despair from my heart and replaced it with something wonderful. I belong here. I belong with you."

"I wish with all my heart that you might stay among us," she answered.

"I will stay. I'll do whatever it takes to become Amish. I don't know what my old life held. I may never know, but God brought me to you. I trust in Him. I believe this love and this faith is His will. It is His gift to me, and I will be thankful all the days of my life."

She wanted to believe as he did but the reality of their situation was far from simple. "John, to become Amish is not an easy thing. What if your old life comes back to you and you must leave us?"

"What if it doesn't?" he countered. "I can't live in limbo forever. I need to belong somewhere. I need to make a life for myself. I want that life to be with you."

She understood his desire to forge his own way

but was it too soon? When would the time be right? Six months? A year? What right did she have to tell him to wait? He was certain of his love and of God's plan for him.

Selfish or not, it was the same plan Karen prayed John would follow for she wanted him in her life as much as she'd ever wanted anything.

The sound of the barn door opening signaled the boys were returning. Reluctantly, she stepped out of John's embrace. "I must go in."

He nodded. *"Guten nacht, meim glay hotsli."*

His little heart. She liked the sound of that. "Good night to you, too, John."

She entered the house and climbed the staircase with measured steps that belied the happiness inside her. Pushing aside her doubts, she relived the moment in his arms. With one kiss John had made this the most wonderful Christmas ever. He loved her.

Karen's happiness carried her through Christmas morning with a smile that wouldn't fade. The snow had stopped and the sun shone bright above a glittering world. Glancing out the window, Karen thought if someone could see inside her heart it must look the same.

Surely there was a sparkling and beautiful wonderland where an ordinary heart had resided only the day before. If not for a small dark cloud of doubt and worry that hovered in the background it would be perfect.

After a morning spent in respectful prayer, the entire family pitched in to get ready for the Christmas feast. When Nettie, Elam and Katie arrived, Anna quickly took over the care of baby Rachel. Less than an hour later, Eli's brother, Carl, and his family arrived, disgorging eight more cousins along with Aunt Jean from the bulging buggy. Soon the house was filled with the smell of baking meats and pies and happy voices.

As the women took over the kitchen, the men took over the sitting room. Karen glanced frequently through the doorway wondering if John felt uncomfortable among her family, but she need not have worried. Once, when she checked on him, he caught her eye and winked then proceeded to jump several of her father's checkers to the hoots of the onlookers.

Noah grinned at everyone. "I told you he is a *goot* player."

It wasn't until the guests left in the late afternoon that Karen tried to steal a few minutes alone with John. Her father and brothers had gone out to start the evening chores. John made to follow then, but Karen quickly asked him to help her put away the extra table leaves.

When her family was out of sight, John swooped in for a quick kiss. It was too brief as far as Karen was concerned, but she recognized his restraint and admired him for it. Part of her longed to bask in the glow of his love and believe everything would work out for them. Another part of her knew her happiness could shatter at any moment. She had spent her life listening to her practical side, but just for today she silenced those doubts and gave thanks to God for the precious gift of a Christmas day spent with the man she loved.

He said, "I'm going to miss you tomorrow."

"We'll only be gone three days. Besides, Papa is leaving Jacob in charge of the farm while we're gone so you'll have him to keep you company."

"Jacob's a nice kid, but I'd much rather spend time with you."

She cupped his cheek. "I will be back before you know it."

John covered Karen's hand with his own. The happiness that bubbled through him was almost impossible to contain. He wanted to shout from the rooftops that he loved Karen Imhoff and she loved him. He thrust aside the tiny voice in the back of his mind that said he was rushing things.

He said, "I don't know how Amish couples managed to keep their feelings a secret. I'm pretty sure people will take one look at my face and know I'm in love with you."

"If they suspect, they won't say anything. It's

a private matter for young couples, but we are expected to conduct ourselves modestly."

"All right, I'll behave but I wish you weren't leaving."

"It's only for a little while."

"It already feels like forever."

She hesitated, then said, "While we are gone..."

"What?"

"Nothing, I'm being silly."

"No, tell me." He would do anything she asked.

"Keep an eye on Jacob for me. He has been hanging out with a group of older boys. I don't think they are a good influence on him."

"I'll do my best. Don't worry."

She smiled then, a wonderful soft smile that melted his heart. "I won't."

The following morning, John saw them off in their hired car. Anna and Noah were excited as ever. Eli looked uncomfortable at the prospect of a car trip as he gave Jacob final instructions about the livestock. Karen just looked adorable.

As the car drove out of sight, John turned to Jacob. "Would you like some help with the horses this morning?"

"*Nee.* I can handle it."

"I don't doubt it for a minute, but Reuben's shop is closed today so I'm free."

"I don't need your help."

Why was the boy so touchy? Perhaps he had the impression that John didn't trust him to do the work right. "If you don't need me I may go to the library in Hope Springs for a while."

He hadn't checked the NamUs website for more than a week. He no longer expected to find anything, but he couldn't give up his faint hope just yet.

Shortly before noon, John took the farm cart and one of the draft horses and traveled the five miles into Hope Springs. At the library, he checked the missing-persons website and found nothing new that related to him. The vague sense of dread that had accompanied him into the building slipped away.

For weeks he had feared he'd never find out about his past, but that had changed. Now, he worried he'd discover something that would take him away from the life he was building. Away from Karen.

On the trip home, John caught sight of a buggy leaving the Imhoff lane and heading away from town. He was almost sure the horse pulling the buggy was One-Way. Had Jacob decided to give the colt a little more road time?

Karen's concerns and his own gut feeling made him decide to follow the boy. Benny was no match for One-Way's pace and John soon fell farther behind.

When he crested the hill south of the farm the buggy was nowhere in sight. John drew Benny to a stop. Where had Jacob gone? Had he turned into one of the farmsteads? Suddenly, Benny looked east and whinnied. Buggy tracks led into a seldom-used side road.

Giving Benny his head, John let the big fellow lumber down the narrow lane. As they rounded a curve, John saw a dozen young men and buggies lined up at the side of the road. Ahead of them, two buggies sat side by side. An Amish boy with a red cloth in his hand stood in the middle of the lane. With a shout, he brought down his flag. The two buggies sprang forward, as the horses raced neck and neck down the narrow road. One of them was One-Way with Jacob in the carriage.

John watched in horror as the buggies rounded a sharp turn, sideswiped each other and locked wheels. The next instant, he saw the wheels of Jacob's carriage catch the edge of the snow-filled ditch.

The sudden drop broke the vehicles apart. As the other driver raced on, Jacob made the mistake of trying to swing back into the center of the road. He lost control. The black buggy flipped over onto its side dragging the horse off its feet.

John jumped down from his cart and raced toward Jacob, running past the other boys who were frozen with shock. He watched in helpless fear as One-Way floundered in the snow, tangling himself in the traces. Reaching the animal, John began speaking soothing words. He worked quickly to untangle the horse. John didn't dare let go of the horse for fear the animal would injure itself or Jacob if he had fallen under the buggy. He had to keep One-Way still. He called out, "Jacob, are you all right? Answer me."

Two Amish teenagers finally raced up to help. After making sure the boys had a good hold on the horse, John said, "Unhitch him and keep him quiet."

Making his way back to the cab, John peered inside. Jacob lay crumpled on the floor. Fear stole the breath from John's lungs. He climbed through the front windshield to reach the boy. "Jacob, can you hear me?"

Please, Lord, let this child be okay. Do not break Karen's heart with another loss.

Reaching Jacob, John felt for his pulse and was relieved to find it steady and strong. "Jacob," he called softly. "Are you hurt?"

Jacob eyes fluttered open. "I don't think so," he answered in a shaky voice.

"Just lie still." John laid a hand on his shoulder to prevent him from rising.

It didn't do any good. Jacob pushed his hand aside and pulled himself into a sitting position. "What about Henry? Was he hurt?"

John shook his head as he searched Jacob's arms and legs for any obvious fracture. "He didn't tip over."

Jacob struggled to stand up. "What about One-Way?"

Hearing the panic in the boy's voice, John knew he was more concerned about the horse than about himself. "I don't know. I wanted to make sure you hadn't broken your foolish neck."

"I'm okay. Please, check on One-Way."

"Your friends are with him. Let's get you out of here first." The two of them climbed out of the buggy.

Before Jacob could rush to check on his horse John gave him a more thorough once-over. Taking the boy's chin in his hand, he tipped his head to the side. Blood trickled from a gash above his eyebrow, giving him a gruesome appearance.

John said, "You're gonna need stitches. Are you dizzy? Can you tell me how many fingers I'm holding up?"

"Two," Jacob answered correctly.

"Do you hurt anywhere?"

"My head aches, but it isn't bad."

John studied the boy's face and decided he was telling the truth. "Let's see if One-Way fared as well."

As they approached the colt, it became clear

that One-Way was injured. The horse was limping heavily on his right front leg.

Jacob abruptly sat on the snowy roadway. "I have ruined my father."

John approached the young horse, speaking softly. He ran his hand down the animal's leg, assessing the damage. "It's starting to swell. It may only be a sprain, but a horse this young can easily fracture a bone. We need the vet to take a look at him."

A tall, slender boy with glasses spoke up. "My *dat* has a phone in the barn. I'll call the vet."

John nodded and the boy took off. As he did, the other carriage came back and John recognized Henry Zook driving it. His cocky attitude had evaporated. "Jacob, are you hurt?"

Rocking himself in the road, Jacob said, "Why did I do it? Why did I let you goad me into racing? I've ruined my father's best horse."

Henry climbed out of his buggy and came to squat beside Jacob. "I'm so sorry. I never meant for this to happen."

John said, "Henry, stay with Jacob. The rest of you come and help me." The young men followed John and lined up beside the fallen buggy. Together they heaved it upright on the road. The damage looked minimal in spite of the rough landing.

Returning to Jacob's side, John said, "We need

the vet to look at One-Way and Jacob needs to see a doctor. Can one of you take him into town?"

"I will," Henry said quickly.

"I'm not going anywhere until One-Way has been taken care of."

John was quick to disagree. "You're going to the doctor. Your sister will kill me if she finds out I let the horse be seen first."

John approached the horse again and ran his hand down the injured foreleg. Already he could feel the heat in it. Looking at the boys, he pointed to one of them. "Let me have your scarf."

The young man yanked it off his neck and held it out. John packed it with snow and wrapped it around the horse's leg to control the swelling.

"Papa will be so upset with me. What are you going to tell him?" Jacob pinned John with a wide-eyed gaze.

"I will not lie to him, Jacob. You are the one who must tell him there was an accident."

John looked over to the rest of the boys. "This kind of racing must stop. You can see now how dangerous it is. I will accept your word that this kind of thing will never happen again. If I hear about *any* of you racing, I *will* speak to everyone's father and the sheriff."

The young men, looking sheepish and relieved, all agreed there would be no more impromptu contests. After sending Jacob off to see Dr. White, John waited with One-Way until the vet arrived.

That evening, John finished icing One-Way's leg and was securing an elastic bandage when he realized someone was watching him. Looking up, he saw Jacob standing outside the stall. The boy sported a small dressing over his eye and a look of doom on his face.

John patted the horse's neck. "He's doing well. With some rest and therapy the vet thinks he'll be fine in time for the sale. How's the head?"

"I needed five stitches."

John stepped outside the stall and latched the door securely. It was a hard way for the boy to learn a lesson but it could have been so much worse.

"Do you like it here?" Jacob asked suddenly.

"Of course I do. I love working with the horses. I love the way your family has welcomed me in. I love…" John stopped, realizing how close he'd just come to revealing his secret.

"You love my sister."

Turning away, John gathered up his supplies. "I'm fond of all of you."

"I did not like you when you first came."

"No kidding? I never would've guessed," John replied, not bothering to hide his grin.

There was no answering humor in Jacob's face.

"The day we found you I knew someone had robbed you and dumped you on our road."

The boy's serious tone set off alarm bells in John's head. He asked, "How did you know that?"

"You had no shoes on but your socks were clean and you had no wallet."

"The sheriff came to the same conclusion." John moved to fork hay into the stalls. A sense of dread uncurled inside him.

After a long pause, Jacob said, "I found something not far from where you were laying. I thought you would think whoever robbed you took it."

John stopped his work. His heart hammered hard enough to jump out of his chest. "What did you find?"

Jacob opened his hand and held it toward John. "I took it. I'm sorry. When you came here and couldn't remember anything, I thought it would not matter that I had kept it. Later, I was afraid to give it back because the sheriff might think I had done this thing to you."

John took several unsteady steps toward the boy and lifted a gold pocket watch from his hand. The cover was finely engraved with the figure of a running horse. John recognized the weight and feel of it in his hand.

When he flipped it open he saw it was an elaborate timepiece that included a stopwatch. Chimes began to play a tune. It was the same tune he'd heard that day in the barn. He looked at Jacob. "You've had this all along?"

Jacob couldn't meet his gaze. He stared at his feet and nodded. "I liked the music. Papa would never let me keep such a fancy thing."

Turning the watch over, John saw it was engraved. His legs gave way. Falling back against the stall door, he slid to the ground. Here was his answer.

He read the words aloud. "To Aaron from Jonathan. Happy birthday, pal."

"I'm sorry," Jacob whispered.

A horrible buzzing filled John's head. He struggled to catch his breath. He could barely wrap his mind around this discovery. "My name is Aaron and I have a friend named Jonathan."

John pressed a hand to his mouth as the implications and possibilities swirled in his mind. He had a name. He had a friend.

He opened the cover and the tune began to play again. It was a waltz. He closed his eyes.

A woman, dancing and swirling, crossed a hardwood floor on bare feet. Her red skirt billowed around her shapely legs as she danced to the tune being played by the watch. Her long blond hair flowed like silk down her back. She stopped suddenly and held out both hands. Clear as day John saw the gold band on her left hand. She smiled. "Dance with me, Aaron."

Pain shot through John's skull. Tears filled his eyes but he didn't know why he was crying. He didn't want to know.

Snapping the watch shut, he pressed his hands to his temples. He didn't want to remember any more.

Chapter Fifteen

Karen stepped out of the car and stretched her stiff muscles, grateful to finally be home. She'd only been away a few days but it felt like a lifetime. While she had enjoyed every minute of her visit with her maternal grandparents, aunts, uncles and cousins, she had missed John terribly. Excitement at the prospect of their private reunion skittered across her skin.

Would he kiss her again?

Jacob stood waiting for them on the front porch. His hat was pulled low on his forehead. Karen waved at him, but he didn't wave back. He stared at his boots as he addressed Eli. "Papa, I must speak with you in private."

That didn't sound good. Karen and Eli exchanged worried glances. What had happened? She said, "Go on, Papa, I will take care of the car."

As Jacob and Eli went inside the house, Karen

paid the driver, took their suitcases from the trunk and herded the younger children toward the house. Noah hefted one of the larger suitcases and struggled toward the steps with it. Anna carried her own but she still wore the same unhappy pout that had appeared shortly after they left their grandmother's home.

Karen asked, "What is the matter, little sister? Aren't you glad to be home?"

"Yes, but I don't want Christmas to be over."

Smiling indulgently, Karen patted her shoulder. "All things must come to an end, even good things."

"I know." Anna shuffled her feet.

Noah stopped and draped an arm across her small shoulders. "Christmas is over, but we can look forward to the horse sale tomorrow."

Giving him a skeptical glance, Anna asked, "Is it really fun? I've never gone with Papa before."

Noah threw up his hands. "Yes, it's fun. You'll see lots of new people and pretty horses. There will be tents set up and they sell all kinds of neat things. Papa will buy us ice cream and good things to eat."

"He will?" She perked up.

"You'll see. It's more fun than market day."

Mollified, Anna followed her brother into the house, begging for more information. "Will I get to choose any flavor of ice cream I want?"

Inside the kitchen, Karen pulled off her black bonnet and hung it along with her heavy coat on one of the pegs beside the door. Disappointment dimmed her happiness. John wasn't waiting for her.

Surely he'd heard the car drive in. Perhaps he wasn't home from work yet. She didn't know if Reuben had his shop open or not. Many Amish closed their businesses and spent the days after Christmas traveling to visit family. Reuben had enough grandchildren that he could easily visit throughout the month of January and not see them all.

Karen tried to console herself with the fact that she would see John soon enough. He rarely missed a meal.

Taking down her apron, she tied it on and began making preparations for supper. She could hear the muted tones of Jacob talking to her father in the living room but she couldn't make out what was being said. Did it involve John? Was that why he wasn't here?

A sudden thought made her freeze. Had John remembered who he was? Had he gone back to his old life?

She wrestled that ever-present fear to the back of her mind where she kept it caged. John wouldn't have left without waiting for her to return. He wouldn't go without saying goodbye. He loved her and she loved him.

She clung to that knowledge in the face of all reason. God had brought John to her. They were meant for each other.

A few minutes later, Jacob came out of the sitting room and she caught a glimpse of his face without his hat on. A bandage and a bruise marred his forehead.

Crossing to him, she grasped his chin and turned his head toward the kitchen window for more light. "What happened to you?"

"I had a carriage accident. I got a couple of stitches, that's all."

Eli had followed Jacob into the kitchen. "The boy and I have discussed this."

"Is John okay? Was he involved?" she demanded.

"John's fine," Jacob answered without looking at her.

"Where is he?" Karen sensed her brother wasn't telling her everything.

"He's working in the barn. I should go help him finish." Jacob made a quick exit, leaving Karen to stare after him.

She turned to her father. "What's going on?"

"Jacob got in some trouble while we were gone. He has told me everything. We will not mention it again." Eli donned his hat and coat and left the house.

Far from feeling reassured, Karen returned to her work with more questions than answers running around in her mind. Perhaps John felt responsible for Jacob's accident and that was the reason he hadn't come to welcome her home. She had asked him to keep an eye on her brother, but she had no illusions about Jacob. If he wanted to seek out trouble, he would find it even with a watchdog.

Jacob and Eli returned a half hour later, but there was still no sign of John. She couldn't help but feel disappointed. Why was John avoiding her?

When supper was almost ready, Karen called Noah in from the living room and said, "Go tell John that supper is ready."

Noah donned his coat and hat and hurried out the door. When he came back a few minutes later, she asked, "Did you find him?"

"*Ja*. He says he is not hungry, but I am," Noah answered as he hung up his coat.

Something was definitely wrong. Karen felt it in her bones.

Supper seemed to last forever, but finally her father rose from the table and retired to the sitting room. Karen made quick work of the cleanup with Anna's help. After wrapping some leftovers in foil, she donned her coat and walked over to the *dawdy haus*.

Stepping inside the front door, she paused to wipe her feet on the braided rug just as John came out of the living room. He held a Bible in his hand. The happy welcome she had hoped to see was missing in his eyes.

Suddenly feeling awkward and uncertain, she held out the plate. "I brought something in case you get hungry later."

"That wasn't necessary."

She gathered her courage as she set the plate on the counter. Gripping her hands together, she faced him. "What's wrong, John?"

He couldn't meet her gaze. "I need to apologize for my behavior on Christmas. I shouldn't have taken advantage of your kindness."

Fear uncoiled inside her, making her pulse pound. "How did you take advantage of me?"

"I shouldn't have kissed you. It won't happen again."

Her heart sank. She took a step closer. "Don't say that."

He closed his eyes. "I need you to leave now, Karen."

"I don't understand. Why won't you talk to me? Why won't you look at me?"

"I had another memory flash while you were gone."

Suddenly, Karen thought she understood. "You remembered her?"

He nodded.

Although she knew she didn't want to hear his answer, she asked. "Who is she?"

"I think she is my wife."

No, no, no!

Karen's mind screamed the denial, but she managed to keep her voice calm. "You think she is, but you don't know for certain?"

"No."

"If you have a wife, why isn't she searching for you?" Karen would have turned the world upside down to find him.

He shook his head. "I don't know."

She had to find some other explanation. She and John were meant for each other. She had known it the first moment she saw his face even though she had tried to deny it.

Stepping close, she laid her hand on his cheek. "You could not kiss me with such tenderness if you had a wife. You are not that kind of man, John. Tell me what you have remembered."

John captured Karen's fingers against his cheek and held them tight as he gazed into her eyes. He wanted to believe she was right. He wanted to believe with all his heart and soul that they were meant to be together, but the evidence was becoming overwhelming.

He whispered, "Let me show you something."

He led her into the sitting room where the watch lay on a table by the sofa. He'd been staring at it for hours. He said, "Jacob found this near me the day I was dumped on your lane."

"It's a watch. Is it yours?" She looked at him in confusion.

"Read the inscription."

Picking it up, she turned it over. "To Aaron from Jonathan. Happy birthday, pal."

Her eyes brightened. "Is your name Aaron?"

"I think so."

"I will have trouble getting used to it, but it is a good name. Why does this make you sad? You have longed to know your own name all these weeks."

He sat down on the sofa. "The watch plays music when it's opened. When I heard the tune, I remembered a woman dancing, holding out her hands and asking me to dance with her. She wore a wedding ring."

Karen laid the watch back on the table and shook her head. "That is not proof you are married."

"What else can it mean?"

She crossed her arms and took a step back. "I don't know, but it is not proof. You had no ring on your hand."

"It could have been stolen." He gazed at his fingers trying to see some evidence that he'd once worn a wedding band.

"What will you do now?" she asked softly. He heard the fear underlying her voice. He knew exactly how she felt.

"I'll take the watch to the sheriff and see if he can trace where it was made or purchased. It's an expensive piece, probably custom-made."

Her chin came up. "It's too late to do anything tonight and Papa will need your help at the sale tomorrow."

She was making excuses and he knew it. She was trying to prolong the inevitable.

So, what would one more day hurt? He deserved one last day of happiness with her and her family, didn't he? Wasn't that why he hadn't gone to the sheriff already? The answers he sought wouldn't change in twenty-four hours. After tomorrow he would resume his search and pray it didn't take him away from the woman he loved.

Glancing at Karen's lovely face in the lamplight he honestly didn't know if he had the courage to leave her.

What could possibly exist in his past that was better than what he'd found in Hope Springs? He'd found peace, happiness and love. He'd discovered a new and simple faith that felt as if he'd lived it forever.

One more day with her. It was all he might have.

He said, "I reckon I can wait until after the sale."

She smiled, but it was forced. "*Goot*. We will have a wonderful time tomorrow. Get some rest. We must leave very early."

She turned away quickly but not before he saw the tears in her eyes. The sight cut his heart to the quick. More than anything, he didn't want to be the cause of her suffering. He'd been foolish to confess his love when he didn't know if he was free. Now, he had hurt both of them.

After Karen left John tried to follow her advice, but sleep never came. The thing he'd longed for had become the thing he dreaded.

What lesson was God trying to teach him?

Just before dawn, a large white pickup pulling a blue-and-white horse trailer rolled to a stop in front of the Imhoff barn. The driver, a young Mennonite from Sugarcreek, helped John and Eli load and secure the horses. When they were ready to leave, Eli and Jacob climbed in the front seat of the extended cab with the driver, leaving John, Karen, Anna and Noah to squeeze into the backseat.

Anna and Noah kept up a running excited chatter. John was glad because it covered the awkward silence that stretched between him and Karen.

He had hoped for one more day of happiness, but there was a pall over the day that couldn't be ignored. He tried to be cheerful for the sake of the children, but each time he met Karen's eyes he knew she was suffering as he was.

The trip took almost two hours. As they pulled into the fairgrounds where the sale was to be held, John saw dozens of Amish buggies along with numerous horse vans, cars and pickup trucks sharing the parking lot. Large numbers of people were already milling about or clustered in front of the tents selling coffee and hot chocolate.

Inside the main building the bleachers were filling quickly as the auctioneer in a booth behind the show ring tested his audio equipment. Long rows of stalls on one side of the enormous building held nearly a hundred horses.

A second long aisle had been set aside for vendors where corn dogs and ice-cream stands shared space with harness makers and nutritional horse-feed specialists. An old-time county fair atmosphere prevailed everywhere John looked. He and Eli settled the horses in their assigned stalls. Cowboys, Amish men and businessmen all filed past looking over the animals going on sale.

Once the auction got under way, John stayed with Eli while Karen took the children for their promised treats. One-Way had made a full recovery. He was the eleventh horse to enter the ring.

When the big colt trotted into the ring and the auctioneer read off his information, including the facts that he was already trained to harness and was a full brother to a stakes winner, John saw a number of English pull out their cell phones. The bidding started low but quickly rose until Eli was grinning from ear to ear.

When the gavel went down on the final price, Eli slapped John on the back. "It is all in God's hands. He rewards His faithful servants. I can't wait to tell Karen. She'll not have to worry about money this year. Where is she?" Eli and John both stood to examine the onlookers crowding around the show ring.

John shook his head. "I don't see her."

"We'll have better luck finding them if we split up. You look by the food tents, I'll check outside and we can meet back here in fifteen minutes."

John left the bleachers eager to find Karen and share the good news of One-Way's sale. Knowing his work with the colt had benefited Karen in some small way lessened the pain he had been feeling.

He left the building to check some of the tents set up outside. The day was cold but not unpleasant and groups of visitors were checking out trailers and horse-care equipment for sale along the south side of the building.

The noise from a loudspeaker drew John's

attention to the fairground grandstands across the roadway. A bugle blared forth the stirring notes of the Call to Post.

A parade of harness horses pulling two-wheeled carts began circling the oval track. The noise from the crowd in the stands grew louder. A race was about to get under way.

The colorful silks of the jockeys flashed in the sunlight as they positioned their horses behind a slow- moving truck with wide gates mounted on the back to keep the horses even. John's pulse began pounding in his ears. His breath came in ragged gasps.

He knew this. He'd seen races like this his whole life. Bit by bit, memories of childhood events tumbled out of the fog that had hidden them. In his mind, he saw himself carrying a bucket of feed toward the stalls. He heard his father's voice calling his name, saw his father dressed in yellow-and-white silks with a racing helmet under his arm walking toward him.

Exhilaration flooded John's body. All his answers were there at the racetrack. He started forward, but stopped when he felt a hand touch his arm.

Karen caught up with John. "Papa found me and gave me the good news. It is a happy day for us thanks to you."

The moment John turned to her, Karen read the truth in his eyes. Her heart stumbled painfully.

He said, "I remember. Karen, I know who I am!"

She tried to speak, but no words passed the lump in her throat.

Excitement poured from him. "My name is Jonathan. Jonathon Dresher. I remember going to a racetrack like that one with my father. He worked there. He was a driver. Karen, I remember him. His name was Carl Dresher. He had the most amazing laugh. He was always laughing at things I did."

The joy suddenly left John's eyes. Karen knew he was looking inward and not at her. He said, "My dad is dead. He died when I was fifteen. My mother—I can't remember her at all. She died when I was little. It was just Dad and I."

"What about your wife?" Karen asked. She didn't dare breathe waiting for his answer.

"Who?"

"The woman you saw dancing."

Confusion flashed in his eyes followed quickly by sorrow. "The woman I kept seeing was Bethany, Aaron's wife. Aaron was my best friend. I loved him like a brother and his wife like a sister. Bethany was Sarah Wyse's sister. That's why I came to Hope Springs, to see Sarah…"

He pressed his fingers to his forehead. "They're

both gone. They died in a car accident the day after I gave Aaron the watch."

"I'm so sorry." Karen laid a hand on his arm in a gesture of comfort.

As if speaking to himself, softly he said, "Everyone I love is dead. No wonder I didn't want to remember. The waltz was Bethany's favorite song. I had the watch made to remind Aaron what a lucky man he was to have found his soul mate."

John turned away to stare at the racetrack. Bowing his head, he wiped his eyes with the back of his hand.

He was grieving for his family and his friends. He'd found them and lost them again all in the space of a few moments. Karen grieved with him and for him—and for herself.

He knew who he was. He knew where he belonged, among the English who raced horses, not among the Amish and their buggies. Would he leave her now? How could she bear it? How would she find the strength to go on without him?

She summoned the most difficult smile of her life. "I'm glad your memory has returned, Jonathan Dresher."

He continued to stare across the road. "So much is still jumbled in my head. I work with a racehorse rescue foundation, but I can't seem to remember who they are or how to reach them."

He gripped her hand and started to pull her

along. "I need to go over there and see if I can remember more. I need a phone to call Sheriff Bradley."

Karen held back. He realized what she was doing and stopped. Giving her a puzzled look, he said, "Come with me."

"*Nee,* I cannot. That is a worldly place. An Amish woman can have no business in a place of gambling."

He stepped close to her. "I don't know what else I'll discover about myself, Karen, but I know I want you at my side. Always."

He didn't mean just for today. Karen suddenly faced the hardest decision of her life. Now that he had discovered his past, he was sure to want to go back to his old life. Could she go with the man she loved into the English world?

Her father was about to remarry. Nettie would make a fine stepmother to the children. Karen wouldn't have to take care of them any longer, but leaving with Jonathan would eventually cut her off from them forever.

Her family would be shamed by her behavior. They would have to shun her. First it would only be her father and the adults of her church, but as Jacob and Noah and finally Anna reached adulthood and took their vows she wouldn't be able to visit with them, or see them marry and raise families of their own.

Could she give up all that for John? She closed her eyes unable to face either future.

He cupped her face between his hands. "I don't want to be where you are not. You've given me everything. You gave me faith and family and love when I had nothing."

"John...Jonathan, I love you so much. You know that, don't you?"

He smiled softly, the warmth of his love shown in his eyes. "I had a sneaking suspicion."

"If you love me you will go now. You will find what you need to know, but I cannot go with you into the world."

A new pain filled his eyes, one she could not bear to look upon. Turning her face away, she said, "I have made a vow to remain true to my faith. I could give up my home and even my family for you, but I cannot turn my back on God."

Jonathan's grip on her fingers tightened. "God will go with us if we keep Him in our hearts. You taught me this."

She laid her hand on his chest. She could feel the thud of his heart beneath her fingers. "Then perhaps that was the reason God brought you into my life."

"I can't do it without you, Karen. I need your strength. You make me whole."

She withdrew her hand and took a step back. "God makes you whole. Go back into the world,

Jonathan Dresher. Remember me kindly for I will never forget you."

"I'll come back to you. I promise."

"If God wills it." Turning away, she walked quickly to where her father stood as tears blurred her vision.

She could not look back at Jonathan. If she did she would run to his arms and leave all that she was behind.

Chapter Sixteen

He had his life back.

Jonathan Dresher stood on the steps of the police station in downtown Millersburg breathing in the cold January air. He'd regained almost all of his memory over the past two days but it didn't feel real.

Jonathan knew where he had been going before the incident in Hope Springs. He knew what kind of work he did. He knew what kind of friends he had. What he didn't know was what he was going to do now.

Two months ago he would've given anything to know the things he had remembered during the past forty-eight hours. Back then he had no idea that finding his past would cost him the most important thing in his life. The only woman he'd ever loved.

He stared down at the plain Amish boots he still

wore. Karen was safe in her Amish community. She had chosen not to come with him into his English world. He understood that. He respected her decision, but that didn't stop the deep ache in his heart.

He had his life back, so why was he standing on these snow-covered steps wishing he were in the snug house on Eli Imhoff's farm?

Because that's where Karen was.

He could see her making supper, talking about a new horse with Jacob, helping Anna with her arithmetic, discussing the Bible with Eli and Bishop Zook, fending off the endless questions of Noah.

Jonathan closed his eyes and held tight to his memory of Christmas Eve and the sweetness of Karen's kiss. Then he locked the memory away for later. Someday, he would take it out and relive that beautiful evening. For now, the pain of his loss was too sharp, too fresh.

Pulling the watch from his pocket he opened the lid and listened to the music. Aaron and Bethany had died together in the car crash. They would never know the pain of being separated. He was thankful for that.

He could see Bethany plainly now. He could hear her laughter, see the love in her eyes when she looked at Aaron. He could hear her beautiful voice raised in song. The memories no longer brought Jonathan pain, only a gentle sadness.

Perhaps one day he would be able to think about Karen without pain, too. He had promised to come back to her, but he hadn't known the kind of commitments he faced in his professional life. He closed the watch, shutting off the sweet sounds of the chimes.

Jonathan had taken over the reins of Aaron's racehorse rescue foundation branch in New Zealand after his friend's death. Once a top prize-winning harness race driver, Aaron had used his substantial earnings to start an organization that cared for injured, abused and abandoned Standardbreds, first in the United States and then later in New Zealand.

A racehorse that wasn't winning often became a liability for those shoddy owners who cared more for money than their animals. It was now Jonathan's duty to see that his friend's work of protecting those horses was carried on.

Would Karen understand? Would she approve of what he did? He didn't see a way he could join the Amish faith and still do his job, which required hours of fundraising, computer use and business travel. Even though he longed for the simple life and faith the Amish shared, he was destined to remain in the English world.

Sheriff Nick Bradley came out of the building

and stopped beside Jonathan. The sheriff settled his trooper hat on his blond hair. "I spent a lot of sleepless nights trying to figure out your story, but I never came close to this. An American, living in New Zealand, comes to Hope Springs to find the Amish family of a dead friend and gets mugged for his trouble."

Jonathan gave him a wry smile. "Sounds like a spiel for a bad movie, doesn't it? There were clues in the things I remembered but I couldn't put them together. I once told Karen there was something missing in the night sky. It was the Southern Cross, a constellation that Bethany said proved God was watching over her life down under."

Nick said, "It sure explains why no one locally could identify you."

"My company wasn't expecting me back until after the first of the year, but I'm sure they're wondering why I haven't been in contact."

"What are your plans now?"

Jonathan shook his head. "There are so many things I need to do. I need to get a new driver's license and a new passport. I need to get access to my bank accounts and rent another car, but first I need to see Sarah Wyse and tell her what happened to her sister. I'm dreading that."

After Aaron and Bethany's deaths, Jonathan had returned to the United States to try and find Bethany's family. He had little to go on, only her maiden name and the name of the town where she grew up. It had been a daunting task, but one he felt he had to complete for her. She often spoke fondly about her sister, Sarah.

Although Bethany deeply regretted leaving her Amish family she knew they would never accept her marriage to Aaron. In her mind, leaving without telling them why spared them the shame of knowing she had left her faith. It was a view Jonathan didn't share and intended to rectify.

He glanced at Nick. "Could you give me a lift to Sarah Wyse's shop?"

"Sure. You know for a guy who didn't have a clue about himself for months you don't seem very excited about getting your memory back."

"There are things I wish I hadn't remembered."

Nick laid a hand on Jonathan's shoulder. "Everyone's life contains moments they would rather forget. I know mine does. It's how we find the faith and strength to face those things that define who we are. Come on, I'll drive you into Hope Springs."

Leaving the outskirts of Millersburg behind, Nick glanced from the road to Jonathan as the SUV rolled past snow-covered fields and farms. He said, "We're still looking for the men who attacked you, but you need to realize we don't have much to go on."

"I'm sorry that I can't remember their faces."

"Knowing what kind of car they stole may help us trace it and we'll check for any activity on your stolen credit cards."

"I imagine the car has been chopped up and sold for parts by now."

"That's quite likely the case. I want you to show me the exact place you were attacked in Hope Springs if you can. It's a long shot, but there might still be physical evidence at the scene. However, unless your witness comes forward with more information for us, finding them is a long shot."

"I understand."

Nick hesitated, then said, "I hope you don't hold it against Sally Yoder that she didn't report the assault. It isn't the Amish way. They forgive such crimes rather than report them. It makes the Amish seem like easy prey to unscrupulous men."

"I don't blame her. I'm just glad that I gave her a chance to get away from the men attacking her. I didn't plan on having my head cracked with a tire iron. Besides, even if she had come forward, she didn't know who I was. She couldn't help identify me."

"Are you *sure* it was Sally?"

Jonathan closed his eyes, trying to relive those moments. The woman had passed close beneath a streetlight across from him. Her open buggy had allowed him a good look at her pretty, freckled face framed by a dark bonnet. "I think Sally was the woman I saw that night, but truthfully, it was her behavior when we met that makes me all but certain it was her."

"Is there anything else you remember about that night?"

"I pulled into the filling station at the edge of town but it was closed for the night. I was putting some air in my rear tire when an Amish girl driving an open buggy passed me. I remember thinking it was late for a young woman to be out, but Bethany had told me about some of her escapades during her *rumspringa* so I didn't think anything else about it."

He recalled clearly the day Bethany had discovered Aaron and himself loafing beneath the apple tree. She had often called Aaron her *geils-mann* with a smile that made it an endearment. That day Jonathan felt a sharp stab of jealousy. They were so in love. Bethany had given up everything to be with Aaron. Jonathan wondered if he would ever know that kind of love.

As she joined the men beneath the tree that lazy summer day, Bethany enchanted them with stories of her Amish life.

Perhaps that was why he felt at home so quickly with Karen and her family, and why it felt so right loving Karen. In his heart he knew there was no one else for him.

Nick asked, "Then what happened after you saw Sally go past?"

"We've already gone over this."

"Humor me. The smallest remembered detail can crack a case. Just tell me again. When did you first see the truck they were driving?"

"I don't remember seeing the truck until it pulled in front of her buggy forcing her to stop. A man got out of the truck and tried to pull her out of the buggy. When I heard her scream I ran toward them yelling something. I think that was the first time he saw me because I'd been squatting down beside my car."

"And you can't remember anything about the truck? The color, the make?"

"It was dark. I was focused on reaching a woman in trouble."

"It's okay. I understand."

"The man trying to pull her out of the buggy let go of her arm and spun to face me. I saw her whip her horse and make a break for it. That's when a second man got out of the truck. He made a grab for her bridle, but she shot past him and got away."

"Thanks to you."

"I didn't do that much. Anyway, at that point, I realized I was facing two lunatics with nothing but my car keys in my hand. I bolted for my car. I guess I didn't make it because that's the last thing I remember. Do you have any idea why they dumped my body on Eli Imhoff's lane?"

"My guess? It was a warning to frighten their Amish victim into keeping her mouth shut."

"I don't understand."

"The Amish are tight-lipped with outsiders, but the news of you being found traveled like wildfire through the community. The blacksmith sign at the end of Eli's lane would have told them it was an Amish farm even if they weren't familiar with the area."

"Are you going to question Sally?"

"I have to. I don't want the same thing to happen to another woman—one who might not be so lucky." Nick's determination to see justice done reverberated in his tone. Jonathan knew Nick would do everything in his power to protect the people in his district and solve this crime.

A short while later they had reached the outskirts of Hope Springs and Nick pulled to a stop in front of the Needles and Pins fabric shop. Jonathan knew his purpose for coming to Hope Springs was about to be realized. After he spoke to Sarah Wyse, he had no reason to remain in the United States. He could go home.

Home was a small apartment above the stables at the farm Aaron and Bethany had owned, but it wasn't where his heart lay. His heart would remain in Hope Springs with a bossy, devout Amish woman named Karen Imhoff.

Nick asked, "Do you want me to come in with you when you talk to Sarah? I've had some experience breaking this kind of news to people."

"No thanks. I need to do this myself." Jonathan took a moment to pray silently.

Please God, give me the right words to say. Let me bring Your comfort and blessing to this woman in her hour of sorrow.

Nick said, "Sarah is a strong woman. Stronger than you know. It will be hard for her to hear her sister is gone, but it's better to know the truth."

"The Amish are strong, aren't they? Their faith is overwhelming in the face of every hardship. I admire them deeply."

Nick laid a hand on Jonathan's arm. "Many of them admire you, too. You'll always be welcome in Hope Springs, Jonathan Dresher."

Karen moved through her days like a woman in mourning. Every corner of the house, every spot in the barn and on the farm carried some memory of her time with John.

Jonathan, she corrected herself. He'd had his life restored. He would be back at his job and with his friends by now.

With sad irony she realized that now she was the one who wanted to forget. She wanted to erase the pain of losing the man she had loved with all her heart.

He had written her one letter in the weeks since he'd recovered his memory. It had been a lengthy missive about his life and what happened before they met. He had signed it, "All my love, John."

She kept it under her pillow and took it out each night. It still brought tears to her eyes but she would never discard it. It was all she had of him.

On the second Sunday following Jonathan's departure, she went through the motions of getting ready for church. She put on her best dress and packed food for the dinner afterward. She went through the familiar motions of living because she didn't know how to do anything else.

Everyone in her family seemed to understand. They made no demands on her time. Instead, they looked after themselves better than they ever had before. Nettie came frequently to lend a hand with the household chores that would soon be hers.

Now, when Karen needed to be needed the most, her family was proving they could do without her.

The trip to William Fisher's farm for services was long and cold and they arrived with only a few minutes to spare. Karen and her family quickly filed into the house and took their places on the wooden benches, men on one side, women on the other. She kept her head down and focused on her hymnbook and prayed for the strength she needed to get through one more day.

Anna tugged on Karen's sleeve and whispered. "Look, there is John."

Karen's head snapped up. She scanned the room around her. Anna pointed to the back row of the men's benches.

It *was* John. Karen's heart hammered in her ears so loudly she thought she might faint. She pressed her hand to her mouth to hold back a gasp.

He was dressed in plain clothes and seated between Reuben Beachy and Elam Sutter. When he caught sight of her, he winked.

She turned back to face the preacher. He had winked at her in church. Jonathan Dresher had come back to Hope Springs. Why? Did she dare hope that he was back for good?

As the singing started, Karen added her voice to the others in humble prayer and gratitude for the Lord's blessing, but her mind was turning like a windmill in a gale. When the song was finished, she endured the longest preaching service of her life.

The minute the final amen sounded, Karen shot to her feet and waited impatiently for the crowd to get out the doors. Outside, she lost no time in locating Jonathan. He was standing by her father and Jacob. The three of them were laughing and smiling like it was any other day. Eli caught sight of her. "Karen, look who has returned."

Jonathan's gray eyes filled with deep emotion when his gaze fell upon her. He said, "Hello."

Karen's voice had fled. She could only stare. The foolish hope that he had come back for her bloomed in her heart.

Anna launched herself at Jonathan and threw her arms around his waist. "John, I knew you wouldn't forget me."

He swung her up to his shoulder and she wrapped her arms around his neck. Smiling at Karen, he said, "I find all the Imhoff women are...*unforgettable.*"

"We've missed you so much." Anna said the words Karen wanted to say but couldn't.

"I've missed you, too." Setting the child down, he cupped the back of her head and dropped a kiss on her bonnet. She clung to his hand, looking up with adoration shining in her eyes.

Noah, hopping with impatience, began peppering Jonathan with questions. "Did you go all the way to New Zealand and back already? Did you fly in a plane? Did you know the sheriff caught the men who beat you up? They'd been stealing a whole bunch of stuff from Amish people."

"Yes, yes and yes, I knew they'd been arrested." Jonathan answered Noah, but his eyes never left Karen.

Realization dawned on her and the foolish hope in her heart withered. He'd come back because of the arrest, not because of her. He would be needed at the trial.

She found her voice at last. "How long are you going to be staying? You must come and have supper with us while you are here."

"I'm going to be staying for a long, long time. As long as God and you will let me."

She blinked hard. What was he saying?

Several of the men who knew him had come up to greet him. Among the handshakes and well-wishes of Jonathan's friends, Karen found herself crowded backward.

"Are you moving here?" Jacob sounded as confused as Karen felt.

Jonathan nodded. "*Ja.* The organization I work for is leasing a small farm not far away. Our need for more stable space in this part of the country is growing because of the recent changes in U.S. horse-slaughter laws."

Several of the local men nodded. One said, "We have heard of this. Broken-down racehorses used to be sold for meat, but now they can't be unless they are shipped out of the country."

Jonathan nodded. "That's right. More of them are being abandoned now than ever. We will take them in, retrain them for riding or pulling buggies and find them proper homes."

"You will need good harnesses for these horses." Reuben Beachy's eyes lit up at the prospect of new business.

"I will. I'll need hay and grain and repair work done on the stables."

"You will need a good farrier, too," Eli added.

"That I will," Jonathan agreed. Looking down at Anna, he said, "I will need my Amish tutor again and I will need to study the Amish ways so that one day I may take the vows of your faith."

A murmur of surprise rippled through the group. Karen's breath froze in her throat as tears sprang to her eyes. He was planning to join her faith. He had declared it in front of everyone.

"After that, I'll need a wife." He looked over the crowd to where Karen was standing.

Anna shouted, "I'll marry you."

Everyone laughed at that, everyone but Karen. Stepping between the men, she grabbed Jonathan's sleeve and pulled him toward the Fishers' greenhouse without a word to anyone.

Inside the plastic enclosure, surrounded by the smell of earth and new plants, she turned to Jonathan and crossed her arms to keep from hugging him. "Is it true?"

He smiled at her tenderly. "Yes. In time, I will marry you, Karen Imhoff. Never doubt it."

Her heart melted with joy. She threw her arms around him holding him as tight as she could. She never wanted to let go again. "Oh, I've missed you so much."

She felt his lips on her forehead. "I've missed you, too, darling."

Holding her away from him, he looked into her eyes. "The moment I reached New Zealand I realized I couldn't stay there. I belong here. With you. With your people. I'm never leaving again."

He pulled her close once more. She returned his embrace with such joy in her heart that she thought she might die of it.

"I dreamed of this," she whispered.

"Wake up, my little heart. I'm not a dream. I'm a flesh-and-blood man who loves the most wonderful woman in the world."

"*Nee,* I will not open my eyes. You will be gone."

"I won't, but I do see one problem with our courtship. Ah, make that three problems."

She looked up to find him smiling. He nodded behind her. Noah, Anna and Jacob had their faces cupped against the plastic walls trying to see in. Karen grinned at Jonathan. "I'm sure they will not object to our courtship as they know you plan to become Amish."

He planted a quick kiss on her lips. "I wasn't thinking about an objection. I thought Amish couples kept their courting a secret. I don't think that's going to happen for us."

She patted his cheek. "I can live with that. Can you?"

He drew her close once more. "As long as I know you will be mine, I can live with anything. God has blessed me, Karen. I will praise Him always."

"He has blessed us both."

Smiling tenderly at her, he said, "I'd like a Christmas wedding."

She smiled back. "I think we can arrange that."

She lifted her face for Jonathan's kiss and gave thanks as her long-hidden love bloomed like a beautiful rose.

* * * * *

Dear Reader,

I hope you enjoyed AN AMISH CHRISTMAS. It's hard to believe another holiday season is upon us already. I want to take this opportunity to wish all of you a very merry Christmas as well as a happy and prosperous New Year. As we get caught up in the frantic pace of holiday shopping and party planning I pray each of us can find a quiet minute every day to reflect as the Amish do on the true meaning of the season.

Christmas blessings to all and to all a good night.

Patricia Davids

QUESTIONS FOR DISCUSSION

1. Karen Imhoff is the caretaker of her family, their surrogate mother. In what way did that role affect her relationship with John Doe?

2. Was Karen right to offer John a place to stay? Why or why not?

3. How did John's amnesia allow him to fit in with the Imhoff family?

4. Would it have been more difficult for John to fit in with the Amish culture if his memory had been intact? Why or why not?

5. Which of the Imhoff children did you identify with most closely? Why?

6. Were you surprised to learn that many Amish buggy horses are former racehorses?

7. The Amish practice of providing homes for their elderly relatives by building "grandfather houses" attached to the primary home seems like a wonderful custom. What problems or benefits do you see with this type of arrangement?

8. The Amish often turn a blind eye to their teenager's behavior during their *rumspringa* or running around years. Is there a lesson to be learned here for modern parents?

9. Karen believed that God had a purpose for placing John Doe in her care. It is sometimes easy to think what we want is also what God wants for us. How can we avoid falling into the trap of following our own will and not the will of God?

10. What was your favorite scene in this story and why?

11. What was your least favorite part of the story and why?

12. Anna felt that God didn't want her because she survived the carriage accident that killed other members of her family. Has there been a time in your life when you felt that God had turned away from you? How did you overcome that feeling?

13. What part of "Amish living" would you find most difficult to maintain?

14. Eli Imhoff tried to keep God first in his

business dealings. How can we keep God first in our own business lives?

15. What part of plain living do you wish you could incorporate into your own life without turning off the electricity?

LARGER-PRINT BOOKS!

GET 2 FREE
LARGER-PRINT NOVELS
PLUS 2 FREE
MYSTERY GIFTS

Love Inspired.

Larger-print novels are now available...

YES! Please send me 2 FREE LARGER-PRINT Love Inspired® novels and my 2 FREE mystery gifts (gifts are worth about $10). After receiving them, if I don't wish to receive any more books, I can return the shipping statement marked "cancel". If I don't cancel, I will receive 6 brand-new novels every month and be billed just $4.74 per book in the U.S. or $5.24 per book in Canada. That's a saving of over 20% off the cover price. It's quite a bargain! Shipping and handling is just 50¢ per book.* I understand that accepting the 2 free books and gifts places me under no obligation to buy anything. I can always return a shipment and cancel at any time. Even if I never buy another book, the two free books and gifts are mine to keep forever.

122/322 IDN E7QP

Name		
	(PLEASE PRINT)	

Address		
		Apt. #

City	State/Prov.	Zip/Postal Code

Signature (if under 18, a parent or guardian must sign)

Mail to Steeple Hill Reader Service:
IN U.S.A.: P.O. Box 1867, Buffalo, NY 14240-1867
IN CANADA: P.O. Box 609, Fort Erie, Ontario L2A 5X3

Not valid to current subscribers to Love Inspired Larger-Print books.

Are you a current subscriber to Love Inspired books and want to receive the larger-print edition?
Call 1-800-873-8635 or visit www.morefreebooks.com.

* Terms and prices subject to change without notice. Prices do not include applicable taxes. Sales tax applicable in N.Y. Canadian residents will be charged applicable provincial taxes and GST. Offer not valid in Quebec. This offer is limited to one order per household. All orders subject to approval. Credit or debit balances in a customer's account(s) may be offset by any other outstanding balance owed by or to the customer. Please allow 4 to 6 weeks for delivery. Offer available while quantities last.

Your Privacy: Steeple Hill Books is committed to protecting your privacy. Our Privacy Policy is available online at www.SteepleHill.com or upon request from the Reader Service. From time to time we make our lists of customers available to reputable third parties who may have a product or service of interest to you. If you would prefer we not share your name and address, please check here. ☐

Help us get it right—We strive for accurate, respectful and relevant communications. To clarify or modify your communication preferences, visit us at www.ReaderService.com/consumerchoice.

LILP10R

Love Inspired®

HEARTWARMING INSPIRATIONAL ROMANCE

Contemporary,
inspirational romances
with Christian characters
facing the challenges
of life and love
in today's world.

**NOW AVAILABLE IN REGULAR
AND LARGER-PRINT FORMATS.**

Steeple
Hill®

For exciting stories that reflect traditional values,
visit:

www.SteepleHill.com